Wonjoon in the Divided Kingdom

The Bell at Shén Dào

Mark E. Verderame

ISBN: 0615579604
EAN: 978-0615579603

DEDICATION

To my family who have encouraged and supported me through my endeavor and with whom makes me complete.

ACKNOWLEDGMENTS

For assistance from Rose Verderame, Shauna Jackson, and Hyun Goo Park whose guidance, knowledge, and support proved invaluable in bringing this book to life.

PROLOGUE

A sphere moves through the darkness of space in the beginning. Collecting gases as it speeds through the great void. When it can contain no more an explosion occurs at its core and light shines forth into space.

Countless other streams of light from similar explosions spring forth in the fledging galaxy. This particular sphere, returns to its darkened state, changed. Containing terrain and rock it falls into an orbit around a massive heated body.

The sphere begins to spin as ice and particles enter at its poles. A blue hue reflects off the sphere into space as the golden sun warms the ice into oceans. The warmth helps the formation of clouds take shape in the bluish sky

Singular organisms enter it and feast upon the poisoness gases left behind from the explosion. As a result the land changes and green plant life takes root.

Higher organisms take shape on the planet and become known as animals. They thrive in the gentle environment, living mainly off plant life. Though, some prey upon other animals and consume their flesh.

One additional organism, the human, appears on the gyrating globe; created to peer into the essence of time. During this being's creation a shard of light, in a mere fraction of a second, enters the human mind. The source of the light originates from the very end of the universe and is sent to give the gift of self-awareness.

This awareness allows them to live creatively and build. In the course of time they come to dominate and conquer the world around them.

But as time moves forward they pursue purely selfish goals which whittle away at their fragile connection with the natural world. In their folly they risk their very existence. It is at this moment in time that our story begins.

It begins somewhere in Asia when the borders that define the cultures in the great continent have become fixed and the languages more distinctive to one another. It begins within a land separated by two seas where peace and prosperity still reign. It is in this land that our story begins.

CHAPTER ONE

Young village children run through the pathways between the small homes. The air, cool and crisp from an early morning shower, begins to change as the sun rises quickly from its slumber into a clear blue sky. Slowly the day heats up as the full power of the sun begins to bake the ground leaving a thick blanket of moisture hanging in the air.

Energy and excitement pulses through the air as villagers prepare for the evening festivities. All the while children play excitedly in anticipation of the nighttime diversions; sometimes to the displeasure of their busy parents.

In the square stands a hand-pump connected to the village well which is near the village shrine. The place between the two has become a gathering place for women in which to rest and gossip as they fill their clay water pots.

The hardy men and women seem to enjoy the preparation taking their time even for the most painstaking detail. They come from a long line of hard working farmers who settled the village over a hundred and sixty years ago. These ancestors of the farmers founded the village when they discovered a nearby spring of fresh water. The pure water came from the melted snowfall on the high northern mountains and filtered through many layers of sediment until it found reached a stream that stopped near the village's main square. At that time, the pure water gurgled to the surface. The village founders constructed a well making it easier to retrieve drinking water. The well, which took two months to complete, stopped seeping because the additional runoff was diverted through an intricate irrigation system to the planting fields near the village.

As the sun makes its way upward, humming birds flit about in the house gardens. Perspiring residents work tirelessly suspending colorful ribbons and banners along poles circling the village square. Laughter from the children becomes contagious which leads to some mischievousness. Small squabbles start between them and their mothers are forced to stop their chores to attend to their children.

The mothers of the unruly children take them home to take care of them as continue preparation for the evening. The children had their attention diverted from play by helping their mothers bake. It was easily accomplished so long as the little ones could sample their work.

At midday the villagers retreated from their chores to seek out some shade or take a swim by the river. The older men gathered under a tarp set up for socializing and the playing of games. They played with the pieces they made by hand of stone and wood and discussed the day's events.

An older boy sat with his father competing in a friendly way with a neighbor, playing a board game that had grooves carved onto a flat square piece of wood. The object of play was to have one player place stones on the board to secure positions while his opponent tried to block or capture his pieces; each one trying to control as much area as possible.

As group of men talked, the conversation turned into a lesson for the younger ones who sat with them about the founding of the village. They told the story of the original three men who established a contract with a local lord at the time to lease these lands that comprise the present village limits.

The agreement stated that the men and their families were to share two thirds of their farming yield with the lord each year. The generous lord, one known for his just acts, agreed to a special request from these farmers which stated that certain parcels of land would become the property of the famers or their descendants if they managed to abide by the terms for seventy years.

The three farmers labored very hard on the land and passed their work ethic to their children and grandchildren. Their grandchildren reaped the reward of all the decades of labor by become rightful owners of the designated parcels which currently make up the boundaries of the village.

This village called Pujon became a unique place in Hana because of this agreement. The lord who granted the agreement was unlike most of the other lords who desired to control their lands and control the people on them. This lord knew that the common man ached in his heart for something of his own and saw no reason why only his life should flourish. This agreement worked so well for the lord that every couple of years he had another village settled with the same type of arrangement. These future villages included many more families and grew much more rapidly than Pujon. This lord made his province, almost unwittingly, the richest in the realm, filled with skilled artisans and productive farms.

The residents of Pujon gained tremendous pride over the years which they demonstrated by making their village exceptionally beautiful. The houses and other structures blended well into the natural surroundings allowing the peopled to live in a seamless harmony with the land.

When the descendants of the settlers of Pujon received ownership they organized a village council and established precepts in an attempt to make a lasting civic peace. The council established only a few rules because they believed in the individual and their right to live according to self-determination.

The first council concentrated their efforts at creating rules that governed the division of land in the village, believing that failure to address the issue would lead to civil unrest in the future. The council members believed that families would grow and divide lands accordingly to these new rules among their offspring. They put in provisions in the village charter and rule book that favored male ownership and encouraged marriage among the locals. Only one stringent rule became created and continually enforced since the founding. It was the prohibition of the sale or leasing of land to non-residents. This was done to keep outsiders from moving there allowing the offspring of future generations to have ample land to start their families.

In their wisdom, the council made one exception to this rule. Outsiders could reside in the village only if they married a local. Those outsiders could not invite any other family members to live with them with the exception of their parents when they reached an advanced age. The original council knew this rule would keep the population under control and give the youth some freedom in selecting a life mate.

The men playing the board games talked about the founding of the village with their children so the little ones would know how to sustain the village's tranquility when they became older.

CHAPTER TWO

At seven o'clock in the morning a Yee-So entered her home and called out to her son who was busy cleaning "Wonja, it's time to collect some water for breakfast." Wonja was the affectionate shortening of the name Wonjoon.

Wonjoon came to the doorway and kissed his mother on the cheek. He took a few steps outside and breathed in the fragrant air of the morning. He turned back to his mother and replied "Okay, Oma, I will get some and then get back home to start the fire."

"Now, hurry along. I too will go to the square to get some vegetables, but you had better hurry first, you know how long it takes to bring the water up the hill," said his mother.

The boy picked up the water pot his mother had left by the door and made his way down a small pathway that turned into a much larger one leading to the town square. When he arrived Wonjoon looked around to see if any of his friends were there. He saw no one he was interested in talking to so he proceeded directly to the well.

The boy pumped water into the pot until it was nearly at the rim. After he filled up the canteen around his neck he returned up the hilly pathway, careful not to spill any water. He knew his mother would force him to return for more if he did. The task was difficult because he had to carry it over an uneven path.

Wonjoon carefully brought the pot inside the house and then went back out to get kindling for the stove. The shutters of the small house were left open to keep fresh air circulating. Only in the winter did they remain closed to keep the warmth the stove generated inside.

Wonjoon added the kindling and dry leaves into the lower opening of the stove and started the fire. He fanned the fire so it would spread to the back section of the stove with a hand fan and closed the door to the opening. When the fire was ready he placed the pot on the stove and waited for it to boil.

A few moments later his mother came through the doorway with vegetables rolled up tightly in her skirt. She started preparation of the vegetables and rice. Wonjoon sat on a pillow and read from his school notebook and occasionally tended the fire; adding more kindling when necessary.

Later his mother, his younger sister Hyun, and he savored a breakfast soup of cabbage and potato. As he ate, Wonjoon daydreamed of the activities to come that day and how much he enjoyed this time of year.

Later in the day Keeyun, his best friend, came over and together they decided to go for a swim in the Haneen River which lay on the outskirts of the village. They knew many of their friends would go there to cool off from the rising temperature. The boys brought with them a backpack that Wonjoon's mother had prepared of vegetables, steamed rice, and melons for dessert.

At the river they basked under the sunlit sky, played and swam in the river with many of their village friends. It seemed everybody in town had come down to the river to cool off and enjoy a break from their chores.

Most of the residents had spent the better part of yesterday and the morning preparing for the evening festivities. With most of the details attended to, the people were ready to relax until evening.

The festivities coincided with the night of the midsummer full moon and had become a long-standing tradition for the village. Each year they took this well-deserved rest after months of hard work to have fun.

Dance contests were set to entertain the people as mutton and rice wine became their feast. Musicians would play stringed instruments as the people watched fireworks and reveled in the magical night.

After two hours of swimming with their friends and playing, the two fifteen year old boys sat down to eat on some large boulders that lay on the side of the river.

"I really would like to see our village from the top of Dusan today," said Keeyun wistfully. Dusan was the closest mountain to the village, although not very tall, it provided an excellent view of the surrounding area. "We haven't climbed it in months together."

"That sounds good, I could go for a hike," replied Wonjoon.

The two cleaned up their lunch remains and buried the waste under a rock. They then crossed over the small footbridge that spanned the river and took a well-worn trail that led to the top of Dusan which was a favorite of the village elders for their morning exercise routine.

The boys hiked for almost an hour until coming to their favorite tree near the mountain top. They stopped and sat in the shade as they drank some water from Wonjoon's canteen.

Looking out from their shaded perch they concluded that this was a much better use of their time than studying. Both of them did not really enjoy the time spent in class and the practicing of calligraphy. Instead they preferred doing something more active such as hunting or fishing. But because custom dictates that children study history and writing until turning the age of sixteen they could do their favorite pursuits.

This year is to be the boys' last in school of which they are truly grateful. The boys promised each other to have more adventures when they finished school.

"Kee," Wonjoon called out to his friend as he stood up. "I wager my last piece a melon in my pack that I can make it down to the trailhead before you." Keeyun had been just about to bite into an apple he had carried when he tossed it into Wonjoon's backpack, stood up, and leapt ahead of his friend onto the trail. As they neared the bottom, Wonjoon jumped from a small cliff to catch up to his friend who had maintained the lead the whole time. Neck and neck they rand until the faster Wonjoon entered the trailhead first.

Wonjoon slapped Keeyun on the back and said between breaths "You almost had me there, Kee but I couldn't let you win. I could never live with you telling others that you beat me."

Both walked slowly back into the village, separating when they came to the pathway that led to Keeyun's home.

"See you later," said Wonjoon "I am sure my mother has some more chores for me to do for the celebration tonight."

"Me, too, there will probably be something needing my attention I am sure," replied Keeyun as he waved goodbye.

Wonjoon enjoyed the walk the rest of the way home and did not rush. He delighted in the varied colors of the gardens he passed on the way. The gardens of Pujon had become quite famous throughout the province. Many strangers came here during the summer months to visit the village and see the gardens. A small inn was set up by one enterprising local for the visitors to spend a night or two.

The gardens attracted many winged creatures, big and small, which flew in haphazard patterns of flight. They provided a symphony of chirping and buzzing sounds to the frequent passerby.

As the falling shadow of night erased the light from the sky hibiscus-scented air slowly drifted in from the fields. The fragrance filled the nighttime air exhilarating the village occupants. These fragrances mixed with the chirping of cicadas dangling from the tree branches lent a special enchantment to the night.

Soon it was time for the evening celebration to begin in earnest. The residents set off fireworks at sunset and the sky turned a colored smoky hue and music wafted through the village as people danced. Indeed, this night held a special power to entice the senses and bring delight to the mind of the young and old alike.

Many hours of merriment passed t until the villagers were ready to put out the lantern fires and douse the roasting pits.

Contented and exhausted they went home full of many fond memories later to be revisited as they dreamed.

CHAPTER THREE

Unlike, most of the villagers, Wonjoon had a fitful night of sleep. Strange images appeared in his dreams that prevented him from reaching a deep sleep state.

This was not the first time during the summer months that he had disturbing dreams. Normally, they began with pleasant and happy memories such as playing and sharing time with friends. Gradually, different and disconnected images took shape and invaded his dreams. This night he had many different images imprinted into his mind; one was of a girl crying in an empty, dark and cold room that seemed so real that Wonjoon believed he could almost touch the objects around her.

His spirit floated like a dragonfly while his conscious-self reviewed each part of the room from the cracks in the wall to the possessions on the floor. The girl had no mattress but slept on some straw that covered a thin flat board.

He moved beyond her room into a bigger one where rice cooked on the stove. The room's floor consisted of rocks and some moldy wooden beams covered by a thin layer of dirt. Some water dripped from the ceiling down into a bucket; as the rain pelted house.

He followed his curiosity and went beyond the walls of the simple dwelling. There, he turned and looked up to see an older woman on the roof who was struggling to patch the leak. She came down the small makeshift ladder she was on to retrieve some more materials before going back up. She plodded through her task knowing of its importance but without spirit or energy.

From his floating soul-body, Wonjoon saw many houses in this colorless town. One noticeable landmark stood out among the ordinary structures. It was a large black obelisk occupying the main town square. This formidable object had a menacing and cold look. Around it was blackened barbed wire which made its' approach impossible to anyone on foot.

The buildings in the town surrounded the obelisk running along the square's perimeter. Small circular windows without glass dotted these buildings. No road in the town was fully paved; instead mud and puddles were everywhere. Near the main square an old mule lay on the ground. It had a lesion on one of its' hind legs making it whine; a call for help that no one answered.

The consciousness of Wonjoon struggled in this dream state; between the world he knew and this strange new one. Wonjoon felt the pain and suffering which caused him tremendous sorrow. Then, his resting body in bed had gripping chest pain. To relieve this emotional pain, his spirit soared upward away from this place. Floating among the clouds his mind grew calm allowing the pain in his physical body to subside.

His body traveled through the landscape until it floated above a small city which had the same type of houses as the town that he had just visited. The only difference between both places was that here, there were countless more dwellings.

This small city had a square in its center similar to the town. It also had an obelisk which was larger by several meters than the one in the town. A dozen large buildings lined the square and small lodges lay just beyond it.

A special shrine, much bigger than his village shrine, was at the end of a wide main road leading away from the square. Upon glancing at the shrine Wonjoon floated through the air horizontally toward it. Inside the shrine, his body rotated gently to a vertical position. While floating inside, he saw that it held the statue of a man and some portrait paintings. Underneath each painting a candle burnt illuminating all the portraits.

Wonjoon left the shrine and went up to the closest lodge building. Hearing noises coming from within, he passed through its' wall to find men and women in the production of lances, swords, and arrows.

He passed from this lodge to another one to find men at desks writing on scrolls, and assistants busily walking about. Moments later he passed through the wall of this lodge into a field where soldiers marched in formation carrying clubs in their belts.

Wonjoon came back to the square and went up to its' main building located in the center. He tried to pass through its' front wall as he had done in the other buildings but it proved impossible. No matter how many times he tried, his incorporeal essence could not gain entry.

This particular blue-gray building had two male guards with upright lances and sheathed swords guarding its exterior. Their faces were gaunt and devoid of emotion. Resolute, they stood, in dutiful protection of whatever lay inside.

Changing course, he floated beyond the square and came upon a small hut near the outskirts of the city. Curiosity pushed him forward to investigate. There, he found what seemed to be the most inviting and warm place around. He floated through its open door in keeping with his upbringing; that one always enters a house from its main entry point. This was a lesson he had remembered from his mother who had instructed him in manners. Curiously he felt that she would be proud of him for behaving well.

Inside, Wonjoon heard an older women's soft but strong voice calling out "Jae, my dear, please come now it's time to rest. We have a long day ahead of us tomorrow. You know your father is too tired to help you with your homework. He needs his rest for work." Jae was short for Jaeyin, the fifteen year-old daughter of the woman. The young girl could not understand that her father, Yoona, was very tired after his day of toil. She had yet to experience the drain on a body that work could produce. After a little more prodding, Jaeyin acquiesced to the wishes of her mother.

Gratefully, Yoona lay down and went off to sleep. He felt the pain of old age mixed with long hours of physical labor and the time-consuming administrative tasks he did for the provincial council.

It was difficult for him being the only male of the e household because the law stated that each family had to contribute equally to the community. Families with more males had an easier effort to fulfill the food contribution requirements. On the contrary, this family found it incredibly difficult to follow the law and still have enough food to stay alive during the winter because the aging father was the only male.

Years ago things were different. Then, the father was a well-respected administrator who performed many governmental tasks. His rank granted the family special privileges. These privileges made their lives much easier than that of the average subject. It gave them access to special marketplaces where a variety of freshly killed game and fruits went on sale.

Then, one day their lives took a turn down a path from which they could not return. A high ranking official mistook a solitary action of Yoona as a personal affront to his honor. Her father had released a small quantity of extra grain to some hungry peasants during the winter months without his superior's approval. When the official learned of Yoona's actions, he accused him of misappropriation and misuse of government properties.

Their lives turned completely upside down. They had to leave their spacious home and move into the tiny house in which they now live. Their life with amenities completely ended for them. The worst injustice was that her father was assigned to work as a laborer and had to contend with back-breaking work six days a week.

Wonjoon saw how tired her father was and her mother's worry for his health and their situation.

"Mami," Jaeyin started out very softly as trying to allow her father to fall asleep "can we go down to the river tomorrow and swim? It would be so wonderful to enjoy the waters and relax on its shores since the weather is so hot."

"I know, my dear Jae that it is such a wonderful idea but tomorrow I must finish sewing the uniforms of the guards. You must also help me after your morning Pon lessons. So you see, there will be no time," answered her mother.

The mother saw the disappointment on Jaeyin's face. Trying to ease her pain she added "But maybe if we work extra hard we can go in a few days."

Minutes later Wonjoon found himself outside the house with Jaeyin talking to some girls. They were discussing what they had learned at their morning Pon instruction. Pon training was important for each citizen no matter how old. Pon taught them the mysteries of their great society and the importance of manual labor. It taught them to respect and honor their divine leader and obey his every command.

Pon Cho Hut, the supreme divine ruler of *Bun Dan*, left them divine instructions. Each subject received one copy of these instructions during their lifetime to keep. Those who accidentally lost or damaged their books received a punishment severe enough to cause fear in the hardest of individuals.

These details were not understood by Wonjoon. He merely observed without any deep comprehension of what he saw and witnessed.

He sensed that the people of the village lived a meager life without enjoyment or vitality. One observation stood out to him. He heard children crying with hunger even as their parents labored to produce food. The crying came as a result of their young bodies failing to receive the necessary sustenance for growing strong and healthy. This proved puzzling to Wonjoon. In his village, the people worked just as hard and had an abundance of food which they brought to and sold in large towns. He did not understand why the efforts of these people were less fruitful than the efforts of the people in his village.

The sound of babies and toddlers unable to become consoled by their mothers became too much for him to handle. He lifted himself up into the sky. Wonjoon raced home in a beam of light. He found himself hovering above his body as it rested peacefully. He lay down on the bed and became rejoined.

Wonjoon suddenly woke up. Because of the disturbing images from his dream he found his clothes dampened with perspiration. The boy knew he could not go back to sleep so choose to take a walk to the town center. When Wonjoon arrived there he picked up a bucket left lying on the ground and walked up to the well to fetch water. With the bucket was half full, he put it above his head upside down and soaked his body giving him some relief from the hot and humid night.

Relaxed, Wonjoon sat quietly at the edge of the fountain as the sounds of the night entered his ears. Listening he became aware that the crickets and cicadas were very noisy this night. For some reason the loud noise made him feel drowsy. Sleepily, he walked back to his house where Wonjoon fell clumsily into a hammock strung up on the outside of the house, oblivious to the world.

During the rest of the night, his dreams vacillated between images of his life here and that of the girl; making his sleep at times again fitful. Only in the morning did the focus of his thoughts change.

CHAPTER FOUR

Hunger woke Wonjoon from his slumber before the morning light had its chance. The boy scrunched his body to the center of the hammock and proceeded to swing it back and forth. When he was high enough he fell out of it onto his hand and knees. Getting down this way had become a game he did since he was eight years old when he accidently discovered the amusing trick while playing in a hammock.

Standing up, he got a whiff of some frying eggs his mother was making for breakfast. She had come outside and seen her son sleeping, as he usually does during hot summer nights.

Wonjoon's mother had already set the table. Eggs, some rice, and a soup awaited him. The emptiness in his stomach compelled him to go inside and sit down at the table. He waited for his mother to take a seat before he began to eat.

"Good morning, son. How did you sleep," asked his mother as she joined him for breakfast.

"Alright I suppose," he replied "But I had a strange dream that woke me."

"Oh," she said contemplating what he meant by strange. But before she could ask, Wonjoon ingested his food like a wolf cub fighting with siblings for the last bite of a kill.

Being very adept at eating with chopsticks, more so than most people, he did not drop one kernel of rice from the sticks as he maneuvered them.

Yee-So looked dismayed as Wonjoon continued to eat quickly. She forced a cough to get his attention. Frowning, she said "Wonja, why are you in such a rush, wouldn't it be nicer to eat calmly and enjoy your food?"

"I know, Oma. I eat too fast. I promise that the next time I will slow down when I eat. But I am in a hurry and must finish my packing." She gave out a conciliatory sigh because she knew that boys such as her son acted much the same everywhere. Nothing could slow them down when their minds were set on something.

As Wonjoon finished eating, Hyun entered the room and walked very sleepily toward the table. Yee-So gave her daughter a hug then handed her a spoon to eat the soup sitting on the table waiting for her.

Wonjoon was going on an annual camping trip with the other boys of the village this morning. The trip had become a much anticipated trip for them over the last few weeks. Many of the village men who enjoyed the outdoors would accompany the boys.

The group's departure left most of the women without their men. This was a time they secretly relished but dared not express to their husbands. When the men were gone the women spent more time together socializing and doing their chores together. With the additional free time this created, the woman would relax and picnic down by the river. They only pretended to become annoyed. Consequently the men felt appreciated by their reactions. But the men knew that the women secretly enjoyed the time apart from them.

Yee-so missed her husband dearly and held some resentment for the women of her age who talked about their husbands during this time. Adding to her discomfort was the worry she had for her son, that maybe some misfortune would come his way, leaving the household without any males entirely.

Not only fear, but also the remembrance of her husband caused this anxiety. Yee-So had known her husband since both were very young. They had been friends a long time before they became romantically involved. Also, their families had known each other going back three generations. This made their connection very special and deep. When he passed away Yee-so thought she would not be able to bear his absence. Though the pain had dulled over time, not many days go by that she does not miss him.

It was just around this time Hyun reached her third birthday that their father died. He succumbed to a bout of tuberculosis that had plagued many of the people in the village during an extremely cold winter. Grief had overwhelmed Yee-So for months stopping her from managing the household as she mourned. Wonjoon took over most of the tasks as he allowed his mother to grieve.

The time was difficult for the family as well as a detriment to Wonjoon's studies. He fell behind in his studies. To catch up at school his teachers made him redo all his class work during his precious summer; much to his consternation.

During the first summer following the father's death Wonjoon's mother began again to manage the household. The warmth and length of the long summer days proved very therapeutic. Eventually she let go of most of her grief and started to enjoy life with her children and friends.

The time arrived for the camping trip to depart. The women went down to the river to see their men off. Yee-So gave her son one last hug. Wonjoon bent down and gave his sister a goodbye kiss and then boarded the raft with his friends

The campers, waving goodbye to their loved ones, pushed off the riverside and began floating down the bank of the River Haneen, from the same spot the boys had swam in the water the day before. They floated down the river a good part of the morning until they came in sight of Mount Woyeungsan. At that point they found an open area ashore to make camp and prepared their backpacks to begin the hike.

A legend existed about this mountain that said those who made a spiritual pilgrim to it would discover something about themselves that would enrich their lives. As the elders explained, during their ride on the rafts, it was the adventure and struggle on the mountainside that revealed insight into the individual who climbed it. Their stories made the camping trip seem even more special to the boys.

Last year Wonjoon attempted the climb with the group but became sick which forced him to return to camp. Wonjoon knew that reaching the summit would be much easier for him this year because he was stronger, bigger, and in better health.

Mount Woyeungsan offered many mysteries to explore, from temples, caves, and lava tubes. Wonjoon hoped they would spend much time examining them. Many go there just to experience some peace and solace for a few days while meditating in these sacred places.

Another legend told of places that moved and changed location. One year a group discovered a secret cave and explored it thoroughly. The next year members of the same group tried in vain to locate that cave to no avail. They were all sure they had gone to the correct spot on the mountain but he cave had disappeared. A year later, one from the original camping party, came upon the cave in the same spot they had searched the year before. The legend says that the mountain decides when and for whom it exposes its secrets; the reason for this still remains a mystery.

Just before the summit, a special shrine, called the Shén Dào, lay which has a bell hanging from the interior. The shrine rests evenly and flat on the mountain which allows any visitor easy access to go inside. The base of the shrine is made of granite stone that goes below the surface of the ground.

The shrine is overrun with vines which are thick, old, and petrified. Those vines run into the shrine and hold the bell in a permanent motionless state unable to be rung.

The *Shén Dào* had become crafted centuries earlier by skilled workers. The bell was unique in that it made two separate sounds when rung. Two clappers made this sound possible. One clapper rang from the inside and the other from the outside. They banged the bell simultaneously on the two opposing sides because they were tethered together and separated by a wooden beam. The bell had a vacuum space between the two shells allowing it to make a double reverberating sound; making it sound something of an immediate echo.

The vines around the bell and clapper kept them immobilized. Sounding the bell was impossible. The vines themselves were lifeless and in a petrified state. Many men from time to time tried to free the bell using sharp axes, swords, or hatchets. Each attempt proved unsuccessful. If they managed to cut away even one, another grew back in less than an hour, much stronger and more resilient to future efforts.

The builder of the shrine made the entire structure with special acoustic improvements. Originally, people all over the province heard the ringing of its powerful sound due to a special acoustics design. The roof was constructed from several overlapping metal pieces facing downward in a concave shape. The floor was made of from solid granite which helped project the sound the bell created.

The *Shén Dào* has not rung for a very long time. The tale of its once mighty sound has become mostly a local legend. Elders throughout the province and realm continued the legend of the shrine whenever children gathered to hear them speak.

Those who have tried, say that not even a rock thrown directly at the bell will make it ring. Instead only a thud comes forth, for the petrified vines have imprisoned the bell denying the people of *Hana* a wondrous sound. The imprisonment of the bell had occurred mysteriously a long time ago. It has remained abandoned and unused since that time.

The boys had a quick snack after their preparation. They set off walking a few minutes later in single file with the leaders in front and behind them. After a problematic four-hour rock scramble up the mountainside, the group of villagers finally saw the legendary shrine. The way proved difficult because for every two steps up they slid down one. The loose shale was everywhere on their path making the ascent very difficult.

The shrine sits at the beginning of solid rock covering this part of the mountain. The location of the summit is about another twenty minute climb up and around many large boulders; some hundred meters more in elevation.

The boys rested for a while and had some food to restore their energy. They explored the shrine and then, took to studying their final route to the summit. They would go up and follow this saddle that would come close to the summit. Next they would climb a well-worn route that circled the summit allowing them to reach it from the northern slope.

With the sun beating down heavily upon their bodies they arrived at the mountain summit. The entire group sat quietly, taking in the majestic unmatched view of their land. They could see, in every direction of the compass, the contours and distinctions of their land. They saw the barren mountains to the north and grassy fields, rice paddies, and forests to the south and east.

The view also meant the group was exposed to the weather elements. As they sat the wind started to pick up and chilled many of the boys. The leaders decided it was time to descend. After walking down a hundred meters they decided to rest a little between two boulders which afforded them some protection from the wind. Here, they decided to finish up any food remaining in their packs so as to gather strength for the rest of the descent. Many had packed fried squid with sticky rice to eat while some had the traditional rice roll with vegetables.

During the mountain descent an older boy named Jiho made a suggestion "Why don't we see if we can free the bell? I have a small hatchet and I know others have camping knives."

Keeyun immediately likened to the idea said "Yes, we could work on a vine or two. Let's try our efforts to one side and see if we can make a difference. Who knows? If we remove one vine it will prove that with more effort we could release the bell from its captivity."

A general chorus of acceptance of the idea went through the group. Only the younger children expressed reluctance at the thought of this activity. The older boys promised to make the attempt alone and let the younger ones rest.

Three village elders watched over the older boys as they worked. They only gave direction when they saw fit. They wanted these trips to bring out the leadership abilities of the older boys hence they encouraged open discussion on most activities.

The elders and boys tried to cut through two vines for more than forty minutes. At seeing the loss of time and daylight, the elders finally put a stop to their attempt and ordered the boys to gather their stuff and continue with the descent to camp.

Disappointed, Jiho and Keeyun protested to one leader "If we could have ten more minutes I am sure we will be able to cut some vines away."

The leader Paku, more interested in their safety, said "A few more minutes will not make any difference. To do this properly you have to spend all day with the proper tools. Then, and maybe then will you get some results. But I am not sure."

Relenting, the last two boys filed in behind everyone else. The descent went much faster than their ascent as gravity worked in their favor allowing them to slide effortlessly down the shale stones. Many boys slid down on their backsides to see how far they could travel before stopping; smiling and laughing at the sheer enjoyment of it.

As they got lower some of the younger boys began to complain of weariness. This worried the elder Paku as he knew that little daylight remained for them to get to their camp near the river. He encouraged along "Come on lads, we are almost back to our base camp. There will be a special meal waiting for us. I am sure you all are hungry and want to eat." The young one nodded their heads dutifully as they plodded along.

Through the careful guidance of Paku the entire group reached the floor of the valley. When they arrived at the campsite the younger boys went immediately to their tents and collapsed on top of their bedrolls. There they would remain until another elder retrieved them for dinner.

CHAPTER FIVE

The surprise evening meal consisted of wild rabbits caught during the day and roasted on skewers. The cook served the rabbits with boiled radish and rice topped with a red pepper sauce. For dessert they toasted cinnamon rice cakes.

Afterwards, the head leader, Han Yip, told the same story other leaders had told during past camping trips. It had become a big favorite among the boys. They knew their leader would tell the story whether they asked for it or not. But they made the pretense of asking him to tell it again. He ceremoniously refused at first, and until sufficiently prodded, began to recount the tale.

As the boys quieted down around the campfire, Han Yip began his story "A very long time ago in *Ilhanung*, the ancient name of this land, a time not much different from the way in which we live today, there was a great lord who resided in a magnificent citadel. This lord was loved equally by those of royal rank and common blood."

"Though most of the people loved him some ambitious men had become dissatisfied with his style of leadership. These men came from descendants of the royal family or were part of the military. They had somehow come to believe that the kingdom had become weak under the great lords guidance. They saw the lord showing much compassion toward his subjects, even the individual with the lowest merit. They believed that gifts should only flow from the lord based upon family blood lines or the accomplishment of some great deed that had some benefit for society."

After a momentary pause, Han Yip continued in a voice using much intonation in his speech. "This powerful group of men sought to usurp the power of the lord through a most despicable method. Secretly they invited all sorts of ruffians and scoundrels into the kingdom to form a band of mercenaries whose sole purpose was to create havoc and anarchy throughout the kingdom in service to these powerful lords. When the king asked for assistance in defeating the band of mercenaries these lords refused."

"This band of mercenaries consisted of men who had once served distant kings or rulers, but were now disgraced for having committed dishonorable acts. Because of their dishonor they resorted to selling their services which led them to becoming instruments of these seditious lords of *Ilhanung*. For them, these mercenaries pillaged and plundered in a haphazard manner to bring chaos and confusion to the lives of the people.

"Many soldiers, from the rule of the great lord, started to become disenchanted with his rule. One day a large company of the lord's soldiers started a general mutiny in the third largest city near the eastern sea. There, they killed relatives and respected scholars from the lord's court. Afterward, they joined forces with the outlaw band in hopes of securing quick wealth and power."

"This larger group of outlaws began moving with impunity through the entire countryside of the kingdom. They attacked border outposts and the lord's mountain garrison up north. They made it difficult for trade as merchants felt reluctant to take chances by sending goods over land routes," said Han Yip to his audience now captivated by the story.

Han Yip took a deep breath and continued "Meanwhile, the common everyday peasant began to despair as they were robbed of their livestock, grains, and other valuables. Under the steady pressure from these outlaws, the people began to hide in the forests of *Ilhanung* located in the central mountainous region of the kingdom. There they dug out several tunnels that were tied together to provide some safety and escape. These tunnels are rumored to exist still today but no one has ever found them. During that time many people decided to live in them and only venture out at night, to check animal traps or secure other provisions."

Han Yip paused for a second and then he raised his voice higher and hit his right fist into his left hand "Back at the royal palace, one day, they received a surprise attack! The great lord had to abandon in the middle of the night the only place he had ever called home. The great lord made his escape through a secret exit built by his great grandfather."

"He went to the forest where he encountered many of his beloved subjects seeking, like him, refuge and safety. With them, he sought out the underground network of tunnels. When some courageous people in that secret lair heard their lord was in trouble, they came to the surface and guided him to safety."

Han Yip took a sip from his cup of green tea. The boys had become very quiet patiently waiting for the head leader to continue. After a small cough he said in a gentler voice "During his forced exile from power, the great lord's heart slowly began to change. Though at first, he felt gratitude for their assistance and compassion for their circumstances of their lives, his desire to regain his power and prestige overwhelmed his character. As the months passed he obsessed on ways of restoring his losses and became emotionally distant and cold from his subjects in exile."

Han Yip remained silent for a moment to consider the course of the story before continuing. Then he said "The loyal subjects did not know what to make of the changes in their once fair and well-loved lord. They failed to understand that powerful men think differently than them. His obsession unleashed an ancient force buried long time ago in the bowels of the planet. It came to the surface when it was attracted to similar energy. The lord allowed his greed to twist his mind in allowing this dark malice to take complete control of him. It made his heart dark, compassionless, and without feelings. As the malevolence in him grew he plotted his vengeance at his brother for the offence of pushing him aside and having no power."

"Through this insidious infestation of his heart and soul, the great lord abandoned all compassion for the suffering of his subjects."

"Some close advisers saw the changes in their great lord and believed he suffered from some ailment. They summoned doctors who tried to cure his strange ailment. But with no clue to his real affliction and they could only witness his transformation. Not really understanding until later what was happening to their lord and prince."

"There, hidden below the surface of the planet, in that sad and lonely place, a shift of sorts began to take place. The people slipped through the shadows behind time which led to their reality becoming distorted. They were led unknowingly into a parallel existence as real as the one they left behind. Both worlds sat juxtaposition to each other but held apart by a dark malevolent force, moving rhythmically in step with each other."

Han Yip paused and showed signs of fatigue. But after a few second he took a deep breath and continued "Soon thereafter, they realized that the threat they feared no longer existed. They came back out to the surface only to find themselves alone. The once bright sun remained shrouded by some mist in the sky. These conditions did not change over time and soon the people considered them to be normal."

"They passed the *Shén Dào* as they left their tunnels. The same shrine we saw this day." The head teacher motioned his arm back up the slopes of the mountain. "But only the shadow form of this shrine existed; no longer real, but an image of their fleeting memory."

"They set out to tame the world around them. A world filled with wild and fierce animals. Absent for them is the beauty of which we take for granted in *Hana*, our land."

"It is said that they struggle to this day for their basic existence and cannot lift themselves up to know the joy of life. Now mind you, this story is just a legend. And to what the exact truth is I am not sure," with those last words he yawned. Drowsiness led him off to his tent for a night's rest.

The boys sat silently around the campfire. When they realized that the tale had ended, they found comfortable positions and lay down.

As they nestled down on leaves and pine, thoughts about the story and its meaning filled their heads. They knew that most legends had some truth to them; making them even more interesting. Charmed by their experiences mixed in with the elder's stories they fell fast asleep only to relive the day's adventures once more.

Wonjoon had not been asleep long when Keeyun woke him abruptly by pushing heavily on his left shoulder. "Wonja, Wonja, I want to go back up there, back to the shrine now. I want to see it under the full moon."

"Tomorrow, Kee. We have plenty of time to go, tomorrow," he said. Wonjoon tried to roll over away from Keeyun. But Keeyun refused to release his hold.

"No," responded Keeyun stubbornly. "I have found a suitable axe and hatchet. Now we will have the right tools to do the task properly," he said insistently.

"Why is it so important and why in the middle of the night. I am tired," responded Wonjoon still groggy with sleep.

"I was just about to fall asleep when a thought occurred to me," replied Keeyun. "I think the shrine will reveal its' secrets only under a full moon, this full moon. So we only will have this one chance. We must go now!"

"Okay, Okay" said Wonjoon as he dragged himself reluctantly out of his bedroll and put back on his shirt and sandals.

"Drink this tea I just made on our dying campfire. It will help you wake up," said Keeyun as he poured some tea he had just prepared. He took a drink from the cup, refilled it, and passed it to Wonjoon. After taking a few sips, a bit of clarity returned to Wonjoon's eyes as the fog in his mind disappeared.

"Okay, we need to go now to get back before sunrise. Let us run and maybe we can get there in an hour," said Wonjoon, finally showing more energy.

Keeyun took off running. Wonjoon startled by the swiftness of his friend, regained his composure and started running seconds later. Wonjoon, being the stronger of the two, quickly caught up to his friend. Together, they ran up the mountain slopes with the backdrop of a golden moon showing them the way higher. This month the moon always seems higher than the other times.

Their spirits became lifted as the movement of a gentle breeze touched their faces and arms. Higher and higher they went until they crossed back out onto the rocky slopes. Occasionally slipping down on rock shale they managed to finally reach their destination.

At the shrine, Keeyun took out the hatchet from his backpack and handed it to Wonjoon. He said "We must try and free one concentrated area. Then, maybe it will make some sound if we hit it a rock. I know if the bell could vibrate a little it will be easier to free the rest of it."

"Yes, that should work. We'd better get started," replied Wonjoon. Keeyun with the axe and Wonjoon with the hatchet cutting proceed to attempt to cut away the vines with initial vigor near a spot below the bell.

After forty minutes of difficult chopping, Keeyun and Wonjoon gave a chorused sigh of relief as they cleared one small area. Wonjoon leaned upright against the bell to catch his breath. For a moment he felt weak and fainted to the ground, hitting his head on a flat stone. A smattering of blood appeared on his temple. He sat up upright immediately and saw his blood made a perfect circle in the middle of this well-rounded stone of which he hit. He picked it up and looked at the *Shén Dào* that was in front of him. Lifting it over his head he threw it with all his might at the cleared opening. The stone hit the *Shén Dào* and it sprung to life giving off a high pitch sound. After the ring tapered off the bell made some humming noise and then went silent."

Looking around Wonjoon noticed the moon was no longer full but crescent shaped at the horizon. Nonetheless, the bell shined under these darker conditions. The vines disappeared leaving the bell completely free. At that moment clouds gathered in the sky and gale winds started to blow. A light drizzle sprayed the boys and they decided to seek shelter, afraid the storm would become stronger.

As they descended the mountain they noticed that the shale was missing and the way was easier to walk because of a much used trail. In the distance they spotted three small huts, two of which did not seem out of the ordinary. Though, the third one was quite different from what they had seen before. Its' uniqueness was a metal roof which Wonjoon felt compelled to inspect more closely. He knocked on the wooden frame of the entrance where a thick dark cloth used as a door substitute hung.

A very old man, evidently blind, came to the door pushing aside the cloth as he did. He inquired "What is it that you want on a night such as this?"

"Kind sir, we are two boys who are lost and are looking for shelter for this night," replied Wonjoon. "Might you help us? We promise to leave in the morning after the storm has gone'"

"You both may enter if you could help and take what things we have left outside so they do not blow away. The boys quickly picked up a few pots, one semi-used candle, and a walking stick and brought them inside.

"Bring in two stumps, too, and put them by the fire," instructed the old man.

"Okay, sir," said the boys as they quickly complied with the request.

The old man pointed to a large rock and said to Keeyun "Child, can you move that over to the door so as to keep the cloth on the ground in place. I am afraid the wind will pick up and send it flying away."

"I will do it, sir," said Keeyun. The old man went inside and waited for Keeyun to return with the rock. The boy placed it right where the old man held the cloth.

"This should keep the wind from entering the house so we may eat in peace," said the old man.

Wonjoon handed the old man what seemed a walking stick and looked around the hut. "Good, good, my sons. That should help us weather the storm. I would like to introduce to you my granddaughter Su-Yun." As he spoke, she came out of the shadow of the fire so Wonjoon could see her clearly. She was a thin girl, smaller in stature than Wonjoon, with long dark hair. Even though her face was covered with ash from starting the fire, Wonjoon noticed her face turn read at her grandfather's introduction.

"Both of you sit down. We have a special meal this evening, made of rice and root vegetables from our garden. We were about to sit and eat before you came. You are more than welcome to share our meal with us," said the old man to both boys.

"Kamsa," said Wonjoon as he slightly bowed. He sat down next to Keeyun. The old man sat on the stump. Using their fingers they ate from a communal bowl. When the food was finished they prepared for sleep.

With their insides full and warm, drowsiness and fatigue overtook their bodies and they fell fast asleep. No longer talking, they quietly inched closer to the fire and lay down. The girl took down some covers that were on a small shelf and put them over the boys. Moments later, comfortable, they fell fast asleep.

Shortly afterward, the girl retired to her bedroll. Only the old man stayed awake listening to the evening sounds from out the window near the door. He remained there for some time, thinking, until he decided things were well and went to bed.

33

CHAPTER SIX

As they slept that night an old monk entered the dream world of both boys. The monk wearing a simple brown robe stood in the middle of a rainy windswept rice paddy. The rain fell hard on them as well as the ground. Through the torrential downpour the old man remained calm, immune to the effects of the weather. No droplet touched him nor did the wind touch his body. The boys saw the feet of the monk playing in a puddle. He stamped his feet, splashing the water to the side and laughed, doing this several times until he saw the boys in front of him and stopped.

The monk looked at the boys curiously, glancing from them to the soft mud which caused them to sink up to their ankles. The monk did not utter a word as the boys tried to free their legs using their hands. Instead, he gave out a chuckle while watching their actions.

Realizing his folly Wonjoon said to his friend "I will try to free you by pulling you." Keeyun extended his hand to his friend who grabbed it and using his fixed position was able to pull him out. Keeyun then fell to his knees in front of his friend, freed from the mud.

Standing up Keeyun said "Thanks, Wonja." After taking a moment to steady himself upright, he turned and said to Wonjoon "Okay, now it is my turn to free you." He pulled hard at first around Wonjoon's abdomen. After getting no result he decided to push him over. After one strong effort Wonjoon fell onto his backside, muddying most of his clothes.

The monk calmly watched the boys stand and brush the mud from their clothing. Without ceremony or introduction he said "I have a story to tell you. It is more a history to recount than a fable told around campfires. I think it will help illuminate the path you need to follow and rid your minds of confusing beliefs that you both hold onto. This is a history about the land of *Ilhanung*, of which we all belong."

Keeyun interrupted "Listen old man, we do not come from this land of myth of which you mention. Instead, we come from a real place called *Hana*. A place we have lived our whole lives and have never left."

"Silence! You have such arrogance for one so unaware of history. Do not interrupt me again." commanded the monk menacingly.

The monk began the story with "Many years ago there lived in *Ilhanung* two princes named Jo Shin and Jo Hut." The monk continued "These two princes were brothers in line to the throne of the royal Pon family. Jo Shin, the first born, laid claim to be the next king."

"Trouble brewed in the land. A distant king sent mercenaries to *Ilhanung*. One band of mercenaries attacked and killed a few trusted nobles and tried to advance against the seaport to the north."

The monk paused as images of that distant time flashed through the minds of the boys. They saw the fighting between the nobles and the mercenaries. These images proved too much to bear and Wonjoon had to step back away from monk to take in a few deep breaths.

The monk undeterred by Wonjoon's feelings continued "The avarice for new lands made the foreign king order one thousand men from his prisons to join the newly created mercenary army. He selected only the most egregious ones; criminals who had committed the most violent acts in his kingdom. This foreign king granted those criminals freedom as long as they served him faithfully for five years. They gladly took the opportunity to gain their freedom and to receive riches from their plunder."

"He ordered them to venture into *Ilhanung* and cause terror and disruption in a prelude for a larger invasion. This mercenary army made its way secretly into *Ilhanung* and divided into ten separate bands. They attacked travelers and farmers in all provinces of the country. The king ordered his soldiers to seek out these bands of mercenaries and to either capture or destroy them. They finally cornered two of the bands in a small valley. The king of *Ilhanung* sent the few survivors to a prison quarry to work for the rest of their lives."

Images again coursed through the minds of the boys as they saw the hard life of the condemned men. The boys saw how the work drained their lives causing them to have an early demise.

"The people, believing they were safe, ventured outside villages and cities. The other eight bands reunited in a hidden location deep in the forest and planned to make several simultaneous strikes. They would wait for the king to make his annual sojourn to his summer palace in the southern mountains. Half the group would attack the king's party while the rest would make its way into the capital city as normal peasants, then attack and burn the royal residences."

"The king traveled with many fine guards and loyal government administrators. The foreign mercenaries attacked the royal party just below the pass that led to the king's summer retreat. Their coach tried to escape but arrows pierced the glassless windows and inflicted fatal wounds to both the king and his queen. The mercenaries allowed no one to escape. By nightfall all of the king's guards and servants were vanquished, while most of the mercenaries survived."

Next the boys bore witness to the suffering of the royal party. They felt the pain and distress of those who survived. The monk continued "Out of fear, the people hid in caves which were deep in the forests waiting for the band to move on. The land fell into chaos as many royals felt cowardice at the thought of confronting this marauding band."

"Then, one day the mercenaries left *Ilhanung* after being summoned back home by their wicked leader. He needed their assistance in repelling an invasion of his land. These murdering marauders never returned but some of them stayed behind because they thought they could maintain the level of fear they had created. The people realized that their numbers were greater now and they could easily capture the remaining invaders and have them executed."

"As the last became safe, frightened peasants came out of hiding. The residents of the kingdom began the long process of restoring their towns and villages to their prior conditions. The pillaging and destruction left a deep scar and made the land vulnerable. This wound ran deep affecting the minds of many people who lived in *Ilhanung*. It allowed a dark influence to make its way into the kingdom and infect the heart of both princes as the death of their father made then vulnerable."

"These two princes contended for the throne. Each blamed the other for the death of their parents, and for the loss and destruction of their land. The invaders had left a terrible gift. They had sowed the seeds of envy which leads to the corruption of men."

"The brothers grew distrustful and decided to remain in two distinctive areas of *Ilhanung*, separated by a sizeable distance."

"Cho Shin went to the capital city to southwest of *Ilhanung* and began the long rebuilding process. Instead, Cho Hut went north and stayed at the royal summer retreat."

"Cho Shin's intentions were obvious because he was designated to be next in line for the throne. His brother set off in secret to usurp his brother's growing power from a fortress near the northern boundaries of the kingdom."

"Cho Hut met the northern lords and landowners and convinced them to back him with promises of obtaining greater lands and titles to the south. Partially out of greed and partially out of envy of the southern lords, they swayed to the side of the young prince. The northern lords believed, and rightfully so, that the southern lords were held in higher favor with the older prince, as they did under his father."

"In turn, Cho Shin gathered the support of the lords to the south promising them special rights of commerce and complete access to the ports for trading, without interference from the throne."

"Both princes planted the seeds envy throughout the kingdom; an envy that would undermine any remnant of harmony that remained after the invasion by the marauders. The seeds of mistrust that the princes planted made its way down to the ordinary subjects in everyday life. Whereby, neighbors began to doubt each other's honesty. These sentiments led to the undermining of civic peace and honest trade. Corruption began in all corners of the kingdom as trust and respect became lost."

"Cho Hut went down a more insidious path, than his brother, to achieve his goals. Deciding that he needed more than just the support of the local lords, he turned to the dark arts. In the northern ice-covered limits of the kingdom lived a monk who had long forsaken the peaceful life. This monk had experimented with the dark passions of the soul and uncovered methods for prolonging life. He lived nestled in a cave surrounded by ice where his body in a state of rot and decomposition became more grotesque with each passing year because death would not release him from his life."

As the boys listened intently, the old man continued "The people near the mountain feared the monk and used the name Conjurer for him. His family name had long been forgotten, even by him. As the stories of the Conjurer entered the court of the northern prince, the desire of the prince to learn the secrets of dark magic grew stronger. Cho Hut believed he could unseat his brother through these powers. He took up the study for three long winter months in the cave of the Conjurer."

"The Conjurer asked for nothing from his student. He knew that changing the land to darkness would be enough reward."

"At the end of his studies the mind and soul of Cho Hut reached madness. The prince became fully enslaved to this dark power and the influence of the Conjurer."

"Cho Hut, with the help of a talented blacksmith who followed in the footsteps of the Conjurer, made an awful discovery. He learned that dark magic could bring metal objects to life. Through a secret incantation cast upon specially made metal, they would achieve movement and be able to repeat actions without further human intervention. Cho Hut set out to make these special objects designed for use in war and other nefarious purposes."

"He made metal sentries that could become placed on battlefields to protect his soldier's ranks. Others he placed as key points to his fortresses for protection. Thousands together acted as a formidable defense. Some became designed as siege weapons able to destroy any fortification."

"He forced many of the peasants to work in mines gathering ore which was only found in great supply along the northern mountainous border. The rest of the people became placed either in the army or as workers in metal forgeries."

"His heart, overwhelmed by darkness, sought out an even greater weapon. He decided to wield his people's fear into a solid force that would bring down a curtain upon the land, extending south, almost to the limits to the capital city itself."

"At the same time, Cho Shin favored the use of politics and law to gain control and unseat his younger brother. He obtained real and contrived evidence alike to support his case against Cho Hut. He was going to show the people that his brother was not worthy and that the people must quickly join together to be rid of this new threat to the kingdom."

"Rumors of the Cho Hut's madness reached the capital city solidifying the support of the people of the south to his brother. A small delegation of lords from the north came to the residence of Cho Shin and asked him to immediately take up the crown. These lords knew that if they did not take a stand behind Cho Shin, their lives and their lands would be in jeopardy."

"The steward of the Capital City, Lee-Hwin, led the group petitioning the prince. He said 'For too long have we not been led. We are a wandering vessel on a great and stormy sea. We ask for you to become our captain, our king, and guide us to safety.' Then he remained bowed in silence for many minutes awaiting an answer."

"Cho Shin's heart filled with compassion upon hearing these words. This honesty allowed him to abandon all vestiges of greed and desire for power. Thus, he became humble. Cho Shin decided his actions as King from now on would serve the people instead of his personal desires."

"Cho Hut sensed the tide turning against him. As the kingdom was about to coronate a new king, he decided to take a definitive step to gain control. The prince to the north knew that if he failed to act, and act quickly, his demise would become imminent."

"Cho Hut summoned the dark forces and machines under his influence. He sent a storm of rainless clouds to enshroud a good portion of the kingdom. The machines, slaves to repetition, systematically destroyed the great northern forest and the villages along the way as it reached the great river separating the north from the south; which is known today as the Haneen. The north became enshrouded in a permanent state of fog and mist. A shadow reaching across all of the northern land has been there ever since."

"The names of these lands changed as the two separated people began to forget one another. The land ruled by Cho Hut became known as *Bun Dan*, while the other under Cho Shin's control became known as *Hana*. For a while the border was fluid and kept changing, with people still able to freely move about. Those people with more optimistic outlooks gravitated to *Hana* while those with morbid and murky tendencies moved toward *Bun Dan*. Cho Hut, on the first year anniversary of the division, sealed the border. Thereby, families with members in both regions became permanently separated and lost contact forever."

"Those that became drawn into the new northern realm fell into a state of gloom and desperation as they regretted their decision. The dark magic fed off their despair and became stronger and more powerful. During the next several months the border became completely impenetrable because of a new dark spell invented by the Conjurer for Cho Hut. This dark magic made the lands invisible to one another."

"To keep the land he coveted intact and make his rule lasting, Cho Hut realized he needed help. He decided on creating a new and different kind of army in addition to his regular guards. This new kind of army was composed of clerics whose sole function was to maintain control of the populace through fear and anxiety. This unholy army was called the Pon Brethren became solely responsible for eliminating compassion from the populace which could undermine Cho Hut's authority and rule. The brethren devised a system of beliefs that encouraged loyalty and service to Cho Hut at all cost."

"Cho Hut called himself Cho Hut, the Great Pon, supreme ruler, divine inspiration, and father to his people. He declared that to die in the service of the Great Pon would allow a person to live exalted in the next life."

"Just before the year anniversary of the division, King Cho Shin marshaled an army together, with the support of the southern Manor Lords, to invade and capture the north. An infamous battle took place on which was known then as Mount Gjongno, but today it is called Mount Woyeungsan."

"The swordsmen and cavalry of the new king began their assault on the day of the second full moon in winter. They encountered poorly fed troops of Cho Hut. These northern troops fought with rudimentary farming tools against a more effective force from the south. Cho Hut, in his avarice, did not supply his army well. He preferred to keep his best weapons and soldiers close at hand and under strict control. When his underequipped army neared defeat, he sent out his slave machines under the supervision of some of his best soldiers."

"This army of machines did not distinguish between friend and foe. It took the lives of many on both sides during the deadly battle. The men of the Great Pon suffered and wanted to surrender. But they knew that if they did, their families would suffer. Hence they fought on; many losing their lives."

"During this battle, the Great Pon arrived on the slopes of Mount Gjongno. There, he called upon the dark forces at the shrine of *Shén Dào,* to bring a terrible winter storm against his enemies. He subverted this holy site that held the lands together and cast a spell on it that persists to the present time."

"Cho Hut chanted 'Chong Erru' until the winds swirled around the mountain and the temperature fell to a deadly cold point for man and beast alike. Soldiers on both sides began to succumb to the bitter weather. Nothing protected them from the blistering winds as shelter could not be found. The land gave out a great shudder and terrible tremble. Then everything went silent."

"Cho Hut and his guards mysteriously disappeared from the crystallized slopes. Vines emerged through the frozen grounds encompassing the shrine completely which remain to the present day."

"Now, the shrine of the *Shén Dào* is the point to come to and from both lands of which you boys, by fortune, have come through. The entrance has lain hidden until the present time and has never been crossed since that fateful battle."

The monk paused in his story, took a deep breath, and then resumed "For many weeks after the battle, many people disappeared from the south. Rumor said they were transported north to work in the labor villages of *Bun Dan.*"

"Cho Hut looked out upon his realm. There, the sun did not fully rise into the sky and the days appeared grayish all year long. The moon, even when full, lost its yellow glow and became faintly lit in the sky."

"Cho Hut went back to the mountain shrine and made that pathway in hopes of using it to invade the south when he felt them vulnerable enough to attack."

"After the division, the people of *Bun Dan* dedicated themselves to working on farms and in factories. The farms never produced much because the soil in *Bun Dan* was less fertile. Though, they were more successful in the factories producing an abundance of weapons."

"Over time the people under the southern king came to forget the loss of their brothers and sisters to the north. Their land prospered under the new king's rule and that of his descendants. The people proved hardworking and creative. They constructed new buildings, temples, and improved their agricultural technology. Art flourished in the kingdom as people started to enjoy the bounty of their labor. The occurrence of crime slowly disappeared as prosperity reached every part of the realm."

"Because of their good fortune Cho Hut was unable to turn the hearts of these people to darkness. The collective goodwill of these people became a protective shell whereby, his malevolence lost all power in the southern realm."

"Cho Hut eventually died. Had he started the dark arts at an earlier age he may have lived longer. But he was a frail boy growing up and had a weakened heart all his life. He left his oldest son, Pon Kwun Yung as ruler. His son lived an exceptionally long life as the dark forces protected him. Kwun Yung spent many years developing new and different types of weapons. He hoped that he could use it someday to destroy the people to the south."

Keeyun asked "Why has he never attacked?"

The monk answered "I don't know why they never attacked. They struggled in the north with many problems and maybe they forgot our existence as we forgot them for a time. Perhaps they are still waiting for an opportunity to present itself. This is a question that I do not know the answer.

"Maybe," said Wonjoon "We may never know what has happened there since the great division."

As he said those words Wonjoon and Keeyun found themselves back inside the home of the rice farmer; waking as the sun lifted itself into the sky.

CHAPTER SEVEN

A merchant ship registered as the HSS Emerald made its way through the high rolling waves of the open sea near the outer islands of *Hana*. The seas became rough as Simon, a sandy-blond haired boy, twelve years of age, slept in one of the berths reserved for important passengers. Simon journeyed to meet up with his father, Peter Fray. His father was a legal Attaché working with the British Governor General on the island of Java. The Governor General was the official representative of the British Crown for colonial possessions in that part of the South Pacific.

Peter Fray had arrived in Java for a specific task. He was assisting in the creation of the legal documents needed for the transfer of the island territory into the possession of Holland. His additional duties were to advise and oversee individual land exchanges with the British subjects and the government of Holland.

Six months earlier, the British Crown had just finished a treaty with Holland for an exchange of colonial territories. Holland was going to take Java and smaller neighboring islands. In return, Great Britain would take the colony of New Amsterdam to consolidate its possessions on the eastern seaboard of North America. New Amsterdam was discovered by the famous Dutch explorer Henry Hudson over a century earlier. The British wanted to bolster their American colonies to counter the increasing influence of the French in the Louisiana and Canadian territories. The British felt that having the entire eastern seaboard in their hands would provide them ample defense in case of French provocation.

The Dutch realized the economic value Java would hold for its trade routes and were very eager to do the exchange. Its' abundance of agricultural products would make it very profitable for Dutch merchants. The taxation on the increased trade would allow Holland and its king to grow in power and influence in this region of the world.

Peter Fray, a graduate of Cambridge, had been managing the delicate legal work for the transfer for four months. He had left his wife and son back in London six month ago and spent most of this time working closely with local officials on deed swaps and land divisions. The work was laborious and difficult at times because he had to satisfy the desires of each subject of British Crown that owned property on the island.

The absence of his family became a terrible burden for him to bear. Peter Fray requested that his family join him. He received the approval of his request three months after arriving. The British Foreign office saw the value of his service and decided to fund the voyage to Java and whichever destination they would choose thereafter. The British government arranged transport of his family and personal items to Java because they estimated that the work might take up to another twelve months.

As payment for his service Peter Fray would receive a sizeable portion of land either in North American or Australia. He had yet to make up his mind which one he preferred.

The travel arrangements for his family were that they sail to Vera Cruz, Mexico from Plymouth, England. Then travel overland and join the HSS Emerald as it anchored off the new emerging port of Manzanillo, Mexico. The merchant ship was scheduled to pick up seedlings of a few Native American plants and some coffee bean plants developed by a local agriculturalist. The coffee plants had become successful in the humid terrain of Central America and would make it ideal for planting in Java.

After Simon and his mother boarded the ship, it set sail northward, to California to pick up some farm machinery that was made at the Spanish mission of San Luis Rey. At this port, Han's mother Lucette disembarked to take a tour of the mission. She met Father Fermin Lausen, a missionary from Europe, well-known for providing education and medical services to the indigenous people of the region.

Unbeknownst to her at the time, she obtained a strain of tuberculosis while visiting the family residences at the mission. Its' effect on her health was not apparent until two days later when they were on the high seas.

Lucette died a few nights later after a severe bout of coughing up blood. Simon attended to her during the night of her passing. He held her frail hand as he sat by her side and prayed for her.

Afterward a crew member escorted Simon to his berth. As he lay in his bed Simon heard her last words repeatedly in his head. "Your father is all that you have now. Love him well." At the time Simon said "I do, mother, I will always love him." He remembered these words and wept as he finally understood her meaning.

The captain held services the next day for Lucette. He said a eulogy while her body remained draped in the banner of the ship. Simon stood solemnly with hands pressed together, the last time he would be close to the body of his mother.

"Here we send into the hands of God this poor boy's mother," said the Captain to the small group which had gathered. "We consecrate the soul of this pious woman in the sight of God to heaven above. While we send her to the ocean's depth we hope she joins her maker this day and finds peace; in the name of God, amen." The captain kissed the Bible holding it with both hands and then touched the body briefly with it.

After the last closing remark, two sailors walked over to Simon and accompanied him forward. The captain reached out and held the boy's shoulder as Simon held on to the end of the banner covering his mother's body. At that moment a sailor moved the portion of the plank near Simons upward. The body of Lucette was lifted up. It slipped out from under the flag into the choppy waves below.

Simon spent the rest of the day looking out from the stern section of the ship before retiring to his quarters at nightfall. The next two weeks were difficult for Simon as he coped with his depression; at times giving upsetting dreams at night.

A fortnight later a storm approached quickly in the early morning hours as most of the crew slept. They woke startled to find their boat receiving a battering from large waves and strong gale winds. Immediately, they went topside to lower the sails.

The preventive measures they took were too late as the ship turned violently on its keel, making it lean towards its starboard side. Seconds later it smacked into an unseen rock outcrop; causing a break in the midsection of the ship. Water quickly rushed into the hull section, dragging the boat lower into the water. As it sank the boat returned upright one final time and then crashed again into the rock outcrop; resulting in the HSS Emerald breaking into two.

Sailors immediately abandoned ship. The survivors in the water grouped together with some ship remnants. There were thirteen in total, including Simon that managed to move safely away from the danger of the rocks and sinking ship.

A sailor in the group saw land through the flash of a lightning bolt and yelled "Land over yonder." He pointed with his arm in the direction of the land for all to see.

They began kicking together in unison toward the island. The First Officer, named Jenkensen, shouted to his men above the sound of wind and rain "Let's go lads! Don't give up. The shore isn't too far off!"

Trusting in their first officer they swam hardily toward the shoreline. They struggled in the water for what seemed an eternity. Thirty minutes later they made it through the dangerous surf. Seconds later, a large curling wave threw them upon the beach. Slowly, they gathered themselves and moved further away from the sea.

Jenkensen ordered everybody to move further inland to get away from the rain that sprayed their faces. Simon turned around to see one of the masts floating up onto the beach. He knew they had escaped a clubbing by getting out of the water when they did.

He turned back to the men walking inland. At that moment his last reserve of energy vanished. He fell to his knees in exhaustion. Jenkensen saw the young Simon kneeling in the sand and walked back and lifted him up. Together they walked, the First Officer lending his body as support to Simon.

At the tree-line they walked up to a small foothill stepping over many fallen branches on the way. At the top they found a few large boulders and sat between them to wait out the remainder of the storm.

The wait was long as the storm lasted all night. By morning the sun was out and shining. The good weather gave no hint to the violent storm the day before. The only signs were downed branches and debris from the ship floating up to the beach.

"You five lads," pointing to the closest five crew members "Begin collecting all that is salvageable on the beach from the ship," said the First Officer.

"I am going to look for some fresh water," said the First Officer to a sailor who had two canteens strapped around his neck and then ordered him "You accompany me."

Jenkensen lifted one canteen from his neck and emptied the last swig of its water. Carrying it, he turned and headed into the forest beyond the rock shelter. The sailor followed directly behind him.

Jenkensen found a stream, two hundred meters inland, in which to fill the canteens. He ordered the sailor to cut a path through the bush back to the beach so they could come and go easily to this water source.

When Jenkensen arrived back at the beach one sailor took it upon himself to start a fire. A few others gathered apples from a nearby tree. The remaining sailors went through all the debris they had rescued looking for useful items or food.

Simon helped in the scavenging. He felt hungry which motivated him to search for any provisions from the ship that had washed ashore.

After everybody had eaten and rested, the First Officer went up to Simon and asked "How are you, lad?"

"Fine, sir" Simon replied "I feel better now that I have eaten."

"Oh good. I want you to stay close to me from now on," he ordered. "As I want to keep you well and intact so I can deliver you safely to your father. We will be going inland soon to look for higher ground so as to get a good viewpoint of where we are."

"Yes, sir; my strength is returning and I should be able to keep up with you all when we start out," Simon said optimistically.

Simon sat as the sailors decided on which things were worth carrying. The First Officer ordered any valuables to be placed in a small sack to be used for bartering later on. The sailors put the silverware and a jewelry box into the bag.

Two bottles of wine were found which had washed ashore. The men drank the wine immediately with the excuse that they needed the bottles for fresh water. The wine helped them relax. The First Officer allowed them fifteen minutes to enjoy their drink before he ordered them to march into the forest.

Two packs were assembled from materials that floated ashore. A sailor added some fabric to make shoulder straps for the packs. When finished the rest of the sailors stuffed them with necessities such as fruit, fabrics, and tools. The First Officer assigned two sailors to carry the packs for the hike inland.

As the sailors doused the fire Jenkensen said "Okay mates, it's time to get on the move. We don't want to lose any more daylight. Follow me up to my fresh water source.

From there we will fill up the empty canteens and wine bottles, and then find higher ground."

At those last words the group entered the forest in single file with Simon, staying close behind the First Officer. Simon took notice of the rich greenery of the forest as they walked. He noted a unique pink flower he had never seen before; even in the royal gardens back in England which were known for their diversity.

After walking through some difficult brush they came upon a well-used footpath which led up one of the mountain slopes. This made all the men feel better as they knew there must be people nearby to have a path so well worn.

They walked up the path for more than two hours until they came to the highest point around; an excellent vantage point in which to see most of the island. Scanning the horizon, the island appeared mostly uninhabited and forested. But on the other side of the mountain they spotted rising smoke.

"Must be some type of village, First Officer," said a sailor.

Jenkensen replied "I agree. I hope they will give us a pleasant reception when we get there. To ensure no problems I want you all on your best behavior."

The trail on the other side of the mountain looked challenging to go down. Realizing this, Jenkensen reckoned they had better rest for now and make the trek in the morning.

"Lads, let us set up a camp here, make some food and rest for the night. The walk to the far side of the island will take several hours. We won't be able to make it before nightfall," said the First Officer.

A sailor prepared a soup made mostly from potatoes, in a large pot they had recovered from the beach. An hour later the entire crew was sitting under the stars and eating. With the soup and some assorted fruits eaten, the sailors dozed slowly off to sleep.

The First Officer selected one sailor to stay awake as guard and rotate the position each hour to all allow all the crew to rest sufficiently. He thought this measure would protect them against any local who happened to see their campfire and come to investigate during the night.

That night Simon had a disturbing dream. His mother and he were walking hand in hand down a path near the house they had lived in, outside of Plymouth. White tree blossoms fell to the ground under a brilliantly sunlit sky. They walked slowly through the meadow as a light breeze quickly changed to a strong wind. This wind carried all the blossoms away.

His mother's hand slipped from his and he saw her fly of the cliff near the house and fall into the ocean below. She sank out of sight leaving only the blossoms visible on the water's surface. She had her hand extended as if asking him to grab her. He ran after her but she eluded his grasp. As he ran the sun disappeared behind storm clouds. More blossoms entered the field and made visibility very difficult. Rain began to fall which changed the color of the blossoms to a dark brown. The rain carried soot and soon everything around him turned black. He ran up a cliff toward a large house in the distance. At the side of the house he looked out onto the ocean and saw the water had turned black.

He turned back toward the house only to find it had disappeared. Instead he saw a doorway that entered a meager hut. He opened the door and passed into a faintly lit room which had a small child crying. As his eyes adjusted, Simon saw a few more small children weeping softly to the side of the room with what appeared to be their mothers lying motionless. Simon felt the anguish of these children as he realized their mothers were not alive. Compassion rose in his heart as he empathized with their loss.

Simon woke up and found his clothes dampened by perspiration caused from the emotions he felt in the dream. He remained awake the rest of the night, sitting up, waiting for dawn; not daring to risk dreaming again.

CHAPTER EIGHT

The group woke at first light. They set out in the direction of the smoke they had seen from the previous day. Three hours of hiking, first off the mountain and then through a fir pine forest, led them to a dirt road. They followed the road westward and came to the small fishing village which produced the smoke.

Some type of festivity was going on in the village. At the edge of the village they spotted a group of musicians playing flutes. Two villagers accompanied them by playing drums made from animal skins. The older children amused themselves by playing with firecrackers. Simon had seen some firecrackers before at Plymouth. Sailors returning from the orient seemed to always have them and demonstrated their use to the amusement of the townspeople. But they were always in scant quantities, not the abundance he saw before him now.

Smaller children ran and played happily as they chased each other through the billowing smoke their siblings created.

Simon thought that they must be celebrating some annual event. He had read once that people of some cultures celebrated harvests when their lives were based solely on agriculture or fishing.

The castaways saw that the village consisted mostly of fishermen. Many boats lay up on the shore or moored in the small bay in front of the harbor which had an empty pier.

Jenkensen felt relief at seeing the pier. He thought it must mean there is regular transport between the village and the mainland.

"Okay lads, let's go into the village now," said the First Officer. "Now remember, be on your best behavior. I want our stay to be uneventful so they will be inclined to help us."

As they walked through the village, word spread quickly of their arrival. They walked quietly in single file as a curious crowd formed around them. Some of the sailors smiled and waved to the people to show they were friendly.

At the village square, not very far from the pier, they met a group of village elders. They explained through animated speech how they had been shipwrecked on the far side of the island. The elders talked in low voices amongst themselves as Jenkensen drew an outline of their ship and the island. He motioned with his arms pointing to the crew and then the mainland across the waters. He believed he had adequately expressed his desire that they wanted to go there.

One sailor retrieved the box of jewels and handed it to Jenkensen. The First Officer took the ring and walked toward the elder who seemed in charge. Jenkensen said "I want to give this ring as a present to your village. In exchange I hope we can receive some food," while handing the ring to the elder and motioning with his hands the actions of eating and drinking.

Another elder came and took the ring from the main elder. He examined it and said something which appeared as an acceptance of its value. He handed the ring back after a small discussion. Everybody had fallen silent to see the elder's decision. After a few seconds, he signaled that food should be brought to the men. A few people left the crowd to follow his instructions.

Because of the elder's acceptance of sailors, the people became very friendly toward them. After a little while everybody got caught up in celebrating; the sailors included. Meanwhile, Jenkensen alone remained formal as he attempted to communicate with the same two elders the crew's desire to leave the island as soon as possible. They made some gestures that tomorrow a boat would take the men to the mainland. This pleased Jenkensen and allowed him to relax for a while and enjoy the celebration also.

It was past midnight when the villagers finally stopped their fun and decided to return to their homes. A few families allowed the sailors use of two empty huts to spend the night. They were small but welcoming as the sailors found some bedding in them in which to rest.

Next morning, the gesturing continued as sailors and villagers alike tried further communication. A large boat appeared on the horizon which solved the question of when the next boat was coming. It turned out to be a large trading boat that made its way around this and other islands during the summer months.

Jenkensen rummaged through the jewelry box mulling over what he could give to the captain of the boat to get passage to the mainland. After his experience in the village he decided he could barter with jewels as sparingly as possible and still get what he wanted. This would help him save the majority of them for the purchase of sea bound passage for the entire crew.

Finally, he decided on negotiating their next step with one small silver ring with a small emerald inset. He hoped this would be enough to convince the boat captain to take them across the strait between the island and the mainland.

He walked to the pier where parts of his crew were talking and then approached the boat captain and shook his hand. The First Officer made gestures to signal his desire for boarding the boat with his men. After a prolonged negotiation, the captain approved of letting them onboard after accepting some jewels and a few personal items of the sailors, such as a knife and smoking pipe.

The boat captain alerted them by pointing to the sun that they would leave in around two hours. Jenkensen felt relieved that their passage was secured. He turned and looked over his crew and saw how disheveled and unkempt they looked. He advised them to hastily secure provisions and clean themselves up. He wanted them looking less haggard to the people on the mainland, believing properly groomed, his sailor would garner more respect and acceptance.

Many sailors went back into the village and followed the First Officer's advice. They purchased some food at a stand in the main square and then worked on mending any torn clothing. A few sailors were able to locate the town barber who cut their hair and gave them a shave.

As they were getting ready to leave many of the villagers came down to see them off. When it came time to board, the sun was directly overhead in the noon time sky. The boat pulled away from the pier and the sailors waved goodbye to their gracious; feeling grateful for having found such hospitality.

As the boat made its way across the water the men took naps and rested. Simon fell asleep as a warm breeze from the south brushed up against his face. His thoughts raced freely and a pleasant sequence of images coursed through his mind.

In this daydream state, he saw wild flowers glistening on a bright summer day. He saw the sun moving through the sky slowly, at a relaxing pace. Then, the images began to change. He saw the horizon become blackened and the flower around him brown and wilted. It happened so fast that it made his heart seem to miss a beat. He opened his eyes and breathed deeply to calm himself down. With the hot light baking his face he slowly forgot these strange images as he peered out toward the mainland that was getting very close.

CHAPTER NINE

It was early evening when the sailors finished their crossing which took more than five hours to complete. The whole time the sea remained calm and peaceful. They saw what they soon would discover was a unique land far from anything they had ever experienced.

The people of this land, in front of them, lived in semi-isolation because their border to the north was mostly impenetrable due to high snowcapped mountains. They conducted trade from two ports to the outside world; one to the south and the other on the western coastline of the country. These ports are administered by the government to control foreign trade and monitor the comings and goings of visitors to their land.

Jenkensen had listened to stories from many sailors back home that had traveled to this part of the world. They told of how ships they traveled on had to register their cargos, crews, and passengers when docking at various ports. One particular sailor he spoke to told him that all passengers of ship were never allowed beyond the ports' trade zones unless they were diplomats. Those diplomats did not receive much freer rein either but were allowed to visit special government reception areas.

As they were almost ready to disembark Jenkensen recalled one particular tale that had become popular about this specific place. The story took place five decades earlier when some intrepid European came to this land and decided to venture inland without permission. The subsequent events of what happened to them remain unknown up to the present day.

Additional voyagers inquired about them when coming here but found no one able or willing to give any specific details about their disappearance; hence only speculation exists back in certain European circles to what happened. Many have agreed that those explorers probably met their untimely end for failing to observe either the laws or local customs of this land.

This story worried Jenkensen and he hoped to avoid any unpleasantness during their stay. As these thoughts went through his mind, he noticed Simon was reviewing a small map from a chart book he had recovered at the beach of their shipwreck.

"Look at this map, Commander," a sailor named Serge called out. Serge was looking over Simon's shoulder at the chart book. "This is the best description of this part of the world but it seems nothing indicates where a port city may be. I suppose the southern tip around here would be a good place to make a useful port," he said pointing to the map.

The sailor took the book away from Simon and walked over to the First Officer. Pointing to the map, Serge said "You see, I think we are landing somewhere near here. Our route will have to go inland and then we will have to find some road that goes south."

"I agree, we need to have the locals direct us to a port from which we would have the best possibility of ships taking long voyages," responded Jenkensen. "Then, we can negotiate a passage away from here and finally make it to Java."

These navigational charts were copied from the original drawings of that fated scouting mission over five decades earlier. The drawings were added to the nautical library at the University of Cambridge. The naval and merchant forces frequently consulted and copied the charts, stored there, before venturing on long sea voyages. Serge made a mental note to begin recording the terrain of this land in a journal. Then, he could possibly make a contribution of these notes to the library back home. In this way Serge hoped to gain some notoriety and perhaps elevate his career.

Simon retrieved the book and glanced again at the page outlining the coastal sections of the peninsula which jutted out from the Asian continent. Serge asked Simon "Why do you think the cartographer made no indications of towns and other ports?"

Before Simon could venture a guess, Serge answered his own question. He said "When this happens it means the cartographer never sets foot on land. Either the captain or guests on the ship were worried about landing on the mainland during the survey of the land. They did exactly what we did and went to a small island such as the one we just left." He concluded that that the cartographer lacked time to map out the exact details of the inland terrain. That is why only the coastline is properly represented.

For some reason, this peaceful and apparently beautiful land did not appear inviting to Simon. Instead he felt troubled for reasons he could not understand. This mysterious lack of description and detail was partly to blame for his sense of unease. He wondered how different the people would be on the mainland compared to those from the fishing village on the island.

Simon gazed out at the strange land of which they were within a few hundred meters. His mind played tricks as the view before him kept changing. The mist slowly gave way and the green richness of the land overwhelmed him. Small rolling mountains filled his sight. It was a land covered in many lush shades of green. The mist returned and only the immediate shoreline was visible.

Then the mist broke again and he saw rice paddies strewn on a stretch of land leading up to the base of a mountain. Small houses, with smoke rising from some metal tubing poking through their pine timber roofs, became visible.

These new dwellings seemed much different from those of the fishing village on the island. After forcing his eyes to blink to gain focus, he noticed people working in the rice paddies and around the houses. Just seconds before he was not able to see any of these sights. They appeared quickly and he assumed his eyes were playing tricks on him.

"I cannot seem to focus," Simon said in a low voice to no one in particular. "The images just keep changing too fast to concentrate on anything." He turned his gaze back onto the open water because he was starting to feel queasy.

The boat had no pier to dock on. Jenkensen who was at the forward of the boat yelled out "Gather up your belongings men and prepare to go ashore once we are in shallow waters. Then, wade onto the beach, over there," he indicated by extending his right arm to the port side.

The sailors began getting together all their possessions; which they had obtained from either the HSS Emerald or from the island village. Jenkensen went first into the water. The Chief Officer, James Greeves, next in hierarchy after Jenkensen, ordered the sailors to follow by saying "Now, let's go men, we don't want to leave our First Officer hanging from the mast."

Eventually, they entered the water carrying their possessions and then made it to the shore. They climbed out of the murky waters onto nearby rocks. There, they followed a path Jenkensen had started walking near a grouping of trees.

Jenkensen waited for everyone to join him before giving out new orders. "Okay, we need to find our way to a large port. So we'll attempt communicating with the natives. Remember they are not used to us, or we to them. So let us be mindful of our speech and mannerisms when we encounter the locals," he said.

The First Officer then continued "Also, I don't know what type of terrain we will face so it may take some time. Everybody be patient and together we will get through this without too much of a problem."

After those final words Jenkensen and the crew began the next leg of their journey home. Looking back out to sea, Simon could see that the boat had left, going southward along the coast and wondered as to their next destination. As he pondered this question, Simon turned to see he was all by himself. Running for a couple of minutes he was able to quickly catch up to the crew.

They passed a few huts and tried to communicate with the inhabitants. The residents, unable to understand, only smiled at them and offered rice and water. The sailors stopped and took their humble offerings. They felt a deep appreciation for the generosity and mimicked a bow they had seen earlier to show their gratitude.

Serge tried gesturing with his hands about finding a large port with ships. He drew a picture of a ship on the ground to emphasize his point. The resident understood his meaning and pointed west, inland, but really to the far side of the country where another sea bordered their land.

The new arrivals to the land were still walking when Simon heard the chirping of a bird. He turned his head and peered into a bush where the sound originated. There, trapped among the small branches of the bush was a small bird, blue colored with white at its sides.

Simon could see the bird was having trouble breathing and was very still. He thought that the bird had probably become trapped by falling from an overhanging branch of a tree into the bush.

He saw how exhausted the bird was trying to escape from his pinned position. Simon slowly broke some small branches near the ground, and made an escape route for the bird. The bird was frightened by the blond haired boy and did not move. Simon took out a handkerchief from his pocket and reached into the bush. He gently wrapped the bird in the handkerchief and gingerly lifted it out making sure not to scrape the bird's head with any of the bush's sharp twigs. The bird tried to peck at Simon's hand but the cloth prevented it from causing any damage.

Simon stood fully upright and turned the bird around so his beak pointed away from him. A local came up to him with a wooden box. Simon could see that the local wanted him to put the bird in it. After Simon had placed it gently in the box, the man closed the lid. The man walked back to his cart and placed the box there.

Next, he scooped up some dirt from the roadside and picked out two bugs. He smashed both of them in his hand and went back to the cart. The man placed his hand with the bugs below the bird's beak. The bird pecked at his hand and ingested one bug. He placed the other bug in front of the bird and waited.

After a few seconds the bird bent down and swallowed the bug whole. The bird flapped its wings and flew out of the box and landed on the ground on its stomach. The small flight shocked the bird because it did not realize it had recovered. It quickly scrambled to its feet, beat its wings together and took flight. In a few moments it became lost from view behind the trees that lined the road.

Simon felt a sense of relief that the bird would live and sadness since he was sure he would never see it again. These feelings reminded him that he was far from his father. He said a little prayer that his separation from his father would not last much longer.

The crew watched the entire drama of the bird's recovery as if mesmerized. They woke from their reverie when the old man began pushing his cart down the road.

Jenkensen feeling a bit frustrated said "Alright, lads, no more wasting time. Let's get going."

Saving the bird had distracted Simon from the constant pain he felt for the loss of his mother and distance from his father. Now for the first time he felt that he would survive this ordeal and someday be reunited.

Simon said a short prayer of thanks, as was his custom, for what he had seen this day. He believed that if you stopped saying thanks then you would stop receiving. That was something he was not willing to risk.

CHAPTER TEN

As the traveling party walked farther inland many people joined them. The members of the crew slowed their pace so as to show the people they were friendly. The sailors sensed that walking together with the locals would put them at ease.

As they walked, the sailors passed individuals tending their fields or working in front of their homes. Many people stopped to take a break from their chores and waved. Some joined in and walked with the sailors for a while and then, returned home. Some smiled while others simply bowed at them. Children played and laughed. Some older children took to swatting the high grass with sticks to keep themselves amused, as they walked alongside the sailors.

A few older women gave the men some homemade sweetened rice cakes and water. A treat they enjoyed thoroughly, almost as much as the attention itself. The sailors had spent so much time isolated at sea, that their responses seemed awkward when in social situations. But these people showed them real concern for which they deeply appreciated.

Jenkensen looked up at the beautiful blue sky and inhaled deeply, feeling inwardly pleased to have his group of men so warmly received.

Though feeling good, the First Officer showed an outward face of displeasure to his sailors. He knew that as their leader, it was his responsibility to maintain discipline and not have either his crew or he lower their guard. As would any good leader do to maintain discipline, he began barking out orders. "Master Greeves, these tag-alongs have become quite a nuisance. I am afraid our progress for the rest of the day will be severely restrained unless action is taken; and taken immediately"

"What do you propose we do, sir?" asked the Chief.

Jenkensen replied "I believe that in order to separate ourselves from these people, we must leave this main road."

He continued relaying his thoughts "Over there, the land rises and then, turns into a ridge that cuts through those mountains." He indicated the direction by hand. The First Officer had spent the past few minutes contemplating his plan by studying the route with the spyglass they found washed ashore from the HSS Emerald.

Jenkensen had found a map of the area in a local shop of which they passed. After a small amount of bartering he secured it for the price of one jewel from their collection. The map gave the first officer a general understanding of topography and roads in this land. On it he noted a faster route that seemed to bypass the many towns on this road with only some gain in elevation.

He thought that this shorter route would save them much time if they could gather supplies for a night or two of camping. Jenkensen assembled the sailors together to explain his intentions.

The First Officer said "I have an idea. Let's stock up on provisions and follow this route which I have marked on the map. It is a much shorter route which will save us considerable time. Also, because I see no markings of villages on it we will not have constant contact with the locals making us move slower. I think the sooner we make it to this large port outlined on the map the sooner we will find passage taking us south."

Greeves studied the map to understand Jenkensen's thoughts. The Chief saw that the trail would bring them to what appeared to be a large city on the shore of the western sea and not to the south as they had originally thought of doing.

When Greeves made mention of this change in direction Jenkensen replied "This appears much closer and very important to the locals. I think if we go there, we can seek the permission we need for traveling. If we go south, we may not be able obtain the necessary papers from the government authorities to depart this land. Because this port is close to the seat of their government, we may have a better chance to obtain the documents for the voyage south."

"Yes, I agree that this city is important and we may find something that can take us further west. Okay, I see your logic, Commander. We have enough provisions and with good weather it should take us no more than two to reach this main road that goes into the city." replied the Chief.

Simon studied the map while Greeves was talking to the Commander. He saw markings of some structures on the high trail. He curiously pondered what they could be when the commander abruptly took the map from his hand.

"Okay, no more time to waste. We must go now and use as much daylight as we can before we camp," said Jenkensen.

"You're right," Simon said in agreement. "We must not delay. The sooner we begin, the sooner we will get there. Who knows what ship is preparing to embark right now. We must hurry so as not to miss any opportunity."

Without further delay the group of sailors left the roadway and followed a path through the planting field. They entered a forest and walked for ten minutes looking for a trail to lead them higher. Soon they came upon a path which made its way up into the mountains.

Many of their followers continued along with them to the beginning of the trail through the forest. The older people stopped and stared at the backs of the sailors as they walked away. Simon turned and looked at them and sensed apprehension in their faces.

As he started down the path the last of the older people turned and walked away but some of the young boys still found it amusing and followed them for a little while longer. As their interest waned, they too disappeared.

Chief Greeves, who was walking close to Simon, also noticed that their admirers had thinned considerably. His mind turned to their new route and he said "Ah Simon, I believe that the First Officer was right. We've lost much time today. We must go in earnest and try to cover as much distance as we can before nightfall."

"Yes Chief," Simon replied absentmindedly as he was thinking about the local people. He asked the Chief "Did you happen to notice that they didn't seem too pleased that we chose to leave the main road?"

"They did leave our sides very quickly. Maybe they needed to return to work or they left because they were hungry. It could have been a number of reasons they chose to leave us," replied Greeves.

"You are probably right. They just thought our actions were a little bizarre to leave the main road. They don't understand our intentions," added Simon.

Looking forward, Simon could see an elderly man walking alongside the First Officer who had taken the lead. The man was much shorter than Jenkensen but he had strong stocky legs which he had obtained from a lifetime of hiking these trails. His hair was long and white and he had a very round face. As he walked along with the group, a mist developed up ahead where the trail moved to the other side of a ridge. This was no more than thirty paces ahead of them.

The men stopped to consider this midday phenomenon as Simon caught up to them. Glancing around, he saw that it covered the whole terrain ahead of them, making it difficult to see the trail up ahead.

The old man grabbed Simon's right hand. He held onto it as he said some unintelligible words. Then, while lifting his hands toward the mist, he motioned to Simon that he should not go forward. Not understanding his gestures, Simon instead pulled his hand free and walked ahead into the mist. The old man did not follow.

Simon turned around and wondered why he could not see him. Taking a few steps backwards he came of the mist and then saw the man still standing in the same position.

Again the old man pointed to the mist and crossed his arms as if to say 'do not enter'. Simon had seen this gesture before among the people when they refused things.

Simon had an idea. He wanted to see if the old man could enter the mist. He said to him "Here old man, grab my hand." The old man did. He then pulled him forward and brought him to the edge of the mist. Simon reentered the mist and tried to forcibly pull the old man into it also. But he could neither pull his hand nor the old man forward, no matter how hard he tried. Simon turned and realized that the sailors had moved on ahead, out of sight, on the trail. Afraid he would lose them entirely he released the old man's hand and trotted slowly to catch up to the crew.

The sailors sensed a change in their surroundings. Some were hesitant to go any further. One voiced his apprehension by saying "What kind of place are we heading into? It looks not fit for any man to enter."

As Simon reached the last sailor in the column who was named Willers the sailor asked "What were you doing back there, Master Simon?"

"I tried to pull that old man into the area where the mist started. It proved impossible. I had to let go of his hand and quickly rejoin the group for fear I would lose you all," replied Simon.

Willers said "Tis indeed a strange place we've come to that will not let the local people enter. How are we able enter and they not? I hope we made the right decision to come this way."

Simon added "I thought I saw apprehension in the eyes of local people as we ventured down this trail. I wonder what they know that we do not."

Jenkensen had come back to the tail-end of the group to check up on everybody. Listening to their comments he responded "Nonsense, don't make up imaginary things and let irrational fear overcome you." The First Officer knew that worry and fear had no place on their journey.

Jenkensen played on their pride by saying "Why are we letting the fears of superstitious people affect our actions? Do not allow their beliefs to influence you!" He paused as he waited for the weight of his words to sink in. Then he ordered them to move quickly as there were only a few hours left of daylight.

Feeling ashamed of their brief collective moment of worry the sailors said 'Aye' to the First Officer and filed one by one up the trail. As they walked, they tried to stay close together so as to always be in sight of each other.

As they gained more elevation the air turned cooler. No summer heat existed here. Jenkensen took a long rope from a sailor named Atkinson who was carrying one around his neck. He gave the first end of it back to the sailor and had the rest of the crew hold onto a section as they walked for their safety.

Jenkensen asked Atkinson to take the lead. This sailor had to painstakingly feel his way with his feet to ensure each step he took was sturdy. This method slowed down their advance more than they desired.

An hour later, the crew came to a large rock canyon that had some protection from the elements. The fog was considerably less here. No longer needing the rope, they were able to move about freely.

When they got to the end of the canyon they came upon a granite plateau. Rain began to fall and they stretched out the rope again so that each sailor could hold on to it. The wind blew hard against them as they crossed this place where the ground was wet and slippery.

Simon stumbled on a wet rock and lost his footing. Accidently, he let go of the rope and fell to the side. A clump of heavy fog landed all around him. Jenkensen saw the fog cover Simon as he disappeared from sight. Simon began to yell as he started to slip off the ridge to the edge of cliff.

Jenkensen yelled at the men in the front to slacken the rope. Next he said "Okay men. Hold the rope firmly as I descend." He then took off his belt and wrapped it around the rope to slide down.

Jenkensen needed another meter of rope to reach Simon. "Give me a little more slack," he yelled upward. Moments later he grabbed Simon's hand. Then he yelled again "Men, I want you to move to the opposite side of the ridge so you can have leverage to pull us up."

Following Jenkensen's orders, the sailors started to pull the two up slowly. It was difficult for the First Officer to maintain his grip with one hand on the boy and the other on his belt. He asked Simon to grab him around his neck to free both his hands while the crew worked carefully. Finally they succeeded in bringing Simon and Jenkensen back to the top of the ridge.

"Okay boys, move carefully and let's get off this ridge," Jenkensen shouted while he pointed to a rock formation up ahead. "Over there should give us some protection from the weather."

When they arrived at the rocks, they sat down and rested while Jenkensen appraised the condition of his men Jenkensen expected Simon to be in a state of shock. But much to his surprise, Simon was handling his mishap rather well. The boy said "Thanks sir, you saved me. Sorry to be such a bother. But I'm ready to go when you are."

Jenkensen said "You're welcome my lad. Glad you're alright. Okay, let's go men. No point in waiting any longer."

The trail became much easier as the elevation became lower by a couple hundred meters. As Chief Greeves took the lead he stumbled over some wooden poles on the ground, unaware of their existence until he was right on top of them. He saw two crossed poles planted in the ground in front of him with an animal carcass dangling from them. Dried blood covered the rocks below it.

Simon walked over and examined the animal. He could not determine its species because it was severely decomposed. The sailors walked around the animal and then continued on their way in silence. They crossed a few more animals suspended in the same position on other crossed poles. These animals seemed to have been left as warnings to any traveler who dared to hike in these parts. Someone put these warnings here to stop people from using the trail.

"I hope we don't come across whoever left these poor animals here to rot," said Willers.

"Yeah," responded Serge. "Whatever message they are sending, I don't want to learn more about it."

As the group walked some more, the fog began to dissipate. The sun came out and they saw a grassy meadow in front of them. As they walked through it, Simon noted to Jenkensen "I don't hear any sounds now. The wind has died down and the fog has gone. Even though we are crossing a field with many plants there are no bugs or birds which you normally see in summertime. The whole meadow is devoid of sound for some reason."

Jenkensen replied "It must be the altitude. We are probably too high for them."

"I don't know sir. It's the middle of summer and one would expect to find something more than just this grass," interjected Serge into the conversation.

"Look you two," said Jenkensen trying to dissuade them "Try to not let your imagination get the best of you. It is nothing to be concerned about."

Even though Jenkensen made these remarks, he did notice that bugs and insects seemed absent from this place. Jenkensen could hear his beating heart and the sound of the men's feet as they walked on the ground.

The First Officer looked up to see clouds from the north moving toward them. A sense of dread overcame him for a few seconds. He rationalized his fear away by telling himself he was just tired and needed rest. Undaunted, he continued to march along and pushed the worry from his mind.

Finally, they descended into a valley. The sky became brighter and brighter until all evidence of those dark clouds disappeared. In their descent, they heard the slow squeaking of metallic objects; similar to the sound of a pulley lifting large cargo to be placed into a ship's hull.

Below them on a stretch of flat trail was a series of life-size stone soldiers in menacing poses. Some held swords ready to strike while others held lances and spears, ready to fight. Simon thought to himself that these frozen soldiers must have been here a long time, waiting for what, he did not know.

There were four circles of stone soldiers with the outer circle having forty-eight statues. Each subsequent circle had half the amount as the previous one, leaving the inner circle with only six.

When they entered the last inner circle, they found the stones on the ground illuminated. First they started as a pinkish hue and then turned to a fiery red emitting no heat, only light. All of sudden, the ground started to tremble causing most of the party to lose their footing. Each sailor grabbed on to the nearest statue for support.

The statues began to swivel around, tossing each member of the crew onto the ground. Then, the inner statues move closer together as Simon fell into the center of them. Meanwhile Jenkensen and the others landed outside the inner circle

The First Officer began to go back to Simon to protect the boy. But a statue between the two turned violently and knocked him backward.

He called out to Simon "Get out of there; it's some kind of trap. Try and climb over one of those statues."

Simon leaped at one reaching for the shield of one stone soldier thinking he could vault over it. But the minute he grabbed onto it, the shield and the whole arm of the stone soldier detached and Simon fell down.

The center became engulfed in blistering light as Simon was trapped within. The ground gave way and Simon began to fall downward through the stones. Upon his disappearance, the bright blinding light dimmed and went out.

CHAPTER ELEVEN

Simon found himself in the center of a seemingly endless number of red box-shaped metallic objects. To his surprise, these objects began to swivel and turn, without leaving their positions.

The boxes gave off low rumbling and creaking sounds that irritated his ears. It forced him to cup his ears with his hands to block out some of the sound. Looking around, Simon saw that these boxes had metal attachments that looked like the red cranes that flew near the coastal village when they arrived here. These metal attachments swung out away from their boxes and then retracted inward.

The metal boxes and their various attached crane-heads were made in many different sizes and shapes. Some were very thin; almost two dimensional in appearance, while others had the shape of large boxes. Each one had some spear, spike, lance, or other sharp blade protruding menacingly outward. Nothing uniform about them existed except their movement seemed tied together.

Out of curiosity, Simon put his hand on one of the cranes that came only as high as his waist. It moved as he touched it. He jumped out of the way as a sharp blade swung toward his leg. Other metallic cranes, close by, began to move. Somehow they were all interconnected. The movement of one metal object affects the movement of another.

Seeing the danger at the moving metal around him, he stepped instinctively backward to a nearby small crane. He then turned and tried to force it to stop moving. It proved to be an impossible task. Simon had to jump back onto a stone out of reach from the blade as it picked up speed; making its actions more dangerous.

He turned to the left and saw another blade moving toward his head. He ducked down to escape its slicing movement. He lost his balance as a club on the reverse side of the same crane struck him in the chest. He fell to the ground and rolled onto his back. A mace on a chain nearly hit him. He flipped back over to his stomach and crawled to a stone that seemed out of reach of another swinging blade.

He stood up and followed the path downward; the only available safe way to go. He had to stop many times and duck or jump to avoid the continual stream of deadly objects that swung across his pathway. Behind him, the cranes started swinging faster and more fiercely.

Simon heard the sounds from the cranes as they stretched out to hit him. One particular metal appendage made a high pitch sound as it lunged toward him. It then moaned as it missed the body of the boy. Other metal parts screeched from their rust perches as they systematically tried to cut or slice him. Their combined movements kept him moving downward seeking safety.

Simon came upon a path that divided into two directions. He chose what he thought was the wider path to stay clear of the cranes. No sooner had he turned a corner down this path when he came upon a dead end. There, stood a terrifying object with three lances cutting through the air blocking the way. He backed away from that object and ducked just as another crane mounted sword tried to separate his head from his neck.

Realizing his mistake, he fell to the floor and crawled back up the path to where had separated. When he was in a safe position he stood up and made his way down the other path. He made a mental note to take paths that did not have great changes in elevation. Obviously the ones that went down faster were traps.

Simon heard the wind pick up as it moved through this labyrinth. He continued to make his way downward while his heart raced and sweat came pouring out from his pores. The pace he had to maintain was beginning to prove overwhelming and exhausting. The good part of an hour later he was still making his way through this deadly path.

Panting, limping, and bleeding, Simon made one last turn around a large metal box and saw no cranes ahead of him. He took a few steps forward and made sure he was out of harm's way. Kneeling on the ground to recover his breath he turned his head and looked back at the exit. Two lances from two different cranes had crossed and barred the entrance into the labyrinth; preventing anyone from going up.

Simon looked down at his body and saw blood flowing from several cuts. He lifted his head and saw a small pond nearby. Simon walked like an injured lamb to the edge of the pond and took off his shoes and stockings and let the cool water soothe his legs and feet.

The water washed away his blood as he regained his senses. Simon cupped some water with both hands and brought it to his lips to quench the thirst the escape had given him. A little rested, Simon began to study his whereabouts. He saw the trail that led from the labyrinth go down and zigzag to his right.

Determined to keep moving, he followed the trail down until it came to a narrow brook that descended to a pond on his right. Behind the brook was a stone wall twice his size. He stretched out his hand to the wall as a bout of dizziness overtook him. Breathing deeply he shook his head to rouse his body from its stupor. Using the wall for support Simon followed the brook downward until he came to a rocky alcove; the only exit was to return up the same way he descended.

The brook drained away down a hole in the middle of the alcove which was covered by a large awkward rock. Looking up from the rock Simon saw the high stone wall that made a semi-circle around him. He placed his foot on the rock, the only loose one in the alcove. It remained steady and did not budge under his weight. He stepped on top of the rock, turned around and looked back up at his route of descent. The way was shrouded in darkness.

He heard the sound of a loud crack, what seemed to be from the cliff overhead. Water started rushing into the alcove from above as it began to flood. In a few moments the rock from which he stood was the only place not covered by the water.

Simon felt a trembling under his feet. The rock, which seconds earlier was stable, now cracked open into two pieces. Below the rock appeared a large tube where the water drained. The rock crumbled into smaller pieces and fell along with Simon into the tube.

The tube started out straight but then curved horizontally after a ten meters. It twisted and turned as the world became dark. Simon was thrown from side to side as he slid along these turns. His head banged hard against the rock and his spirit was jolted away from his body. As his body fell unconscious his spirit rose through the solid dark granite and out into the open air above.

He flew straight up into the skies above the planet. He sailed farther until the space around him was pitch-black. A star exploded in front of the boy. For a fleeting moment he could see the full dimensions of time and space. Time moved from its rudimentary beginnings forward to the current age. He saw glimpses of history all around him until he came into the land his body now lay unconscious. He saw fleetingly its' divided history until he became enveloped in darkness.

As quickly as these images came, the memory of them became lost. Simon could only remember the star and the sublime beauty of its conception. Suddenly, and without warning, he had the sensation of falling. Simon's spirit vanished into a stream of light as it raced home and instantly entered his corporeal body that lay prostrate on some rocks.

Slowly, Simon sat up and looked around, adjusting to his physical body and its' physical limits. He felt a smooth rock below him and cool water lapping at his dangling feet. Simon was in the middle of a shallow pool on an oval stone that lay in the center which stone pillars surrounded. These pillars were nearly three meters high with thick leafless vines stretching tautly between them.

The water, below him, had a purplish glow. It gurgled slowly over the side making the ground muddy. Simon reached down to find the source of this light; thinking maybe some submerged lantern lay below. His hand came across a metal object. He lifted the object from the water and the pool lost its illumination. The metallic object was shaped similar to a teardrop and oddly enough, did not glow out of the water. Its' surface was rough and completely black. The teardrop object had coarse lines running up and down one side while completely smooth on the opposite side.

Simon decided to examine it more thoroughly later. Wrapping it in his handkerchief he placed the strange metal into his pocket. Jumping off the rock to the dry rock outside the pool he heard a noise. It was the sound of human footsteps echoing off the pillars. He could not tell from which direction they moved because the echo made it seem as if it came from many directions.

The sound of the footsteps intensified as they came closer. He said "I had better be prepared to defend myself, but how?" He looked at the ground and picked up a palm-sized stone.

Tensely waiting for this threat to appear a teenage girl, shorter in stature than him, came running out from behind the pillars. As she entered the area, Simon saw the fear in her eyes and knew that whatever tracked her put him in danger too.

Growls filled the air and echoes of heavier footsteps filled his eardrums. Without seeing Simon, the girl tried to leap across the pool and collided with him. They both landed in the water. Simon lifted himself out of the water and grabbed the girl's arm who was about to continue running. He held her briefly as she turned to face him. Again, he saw the terror in her eyes. A snarl startled him from behind and he let go of her. She jumped from the pool quickly and ran through the pillars on the opposite side.

Simon's heart began to pump hard and called out "Wait, I'm coming with you." He quickly left the pool and followed her as fast as he could.

The fear in the girl made her run fast. Simon who was normally a very strong runner had to muster all his strength to keep pace with her. He managed to get as close to seven paces behind her the whole time they ran.

She abruptly stopped at the beginning of a mountain slope as the columns of stone pillars came to an end. When he reached her, the wet ground gave way under their combined weight. Together they rolled down a shale rock surface which ended at a shallow running stream. He grabbed her hand and said "Let's run through the water. Don't leave the water and our trail won't be so easily followed."

Not waiting to see whether or not she understood his words he grabbed her hand and pulled her along the stream's bank. She fell into the water from the awkward turn her body had to make to follow Simon. He picked her up with both hands around the girl's waist. He released his hands and pointed downstream. "This way," Simon said.

Again, she took the lead. They ran about a hundred meters until they leapt out onto a round rock next to the stream. They jumped from one rock to another. The rocks got bigger and bigger and became the size of boulders. The boy and girl followed their way into a small winding canyon. When they reached the end of the canyon it opened into a large area.

Breathless, the two teenagers paused to rest. They moved to a stonewall barrier that divided the field and leaned against it.

"We are safe now," she said to Simon as her breathing became normal.

"What? How can you be so sure?" he asked, shocked that she spoke to him and he understood.

"They would have descended upon us now if they were still following us. Something stopped them from coming this way. I don't hear their growls now," she responded.

Simon looked at the girl and saw that she was cut and bruised on her arms and legs. Small blood stains dotted her gray smock. He noted that she had short black hair which was tied in a knot.

Simon pushed off the wall and took a good look at the place they found themselves. It was a dark, treeless, rocky are. He looked down as the girl took a seat on the ground and thought there was something familiar about her.

The girl seemed very strong as she looked out into the distance. The dreariness of this place did not weigh heavily upon her, he thought, as it would certainly him.

He bent down to her and extended his hand. "My name is Simon," he started while gazing at her eyes. She looked up at him and stared intently for a few seconds. He thought she was making some judgment about him. It seemed to Simon that her eyes relaxed a little after she determined he posed no threat.

"What is your name?" he asked.

She stood up and bowed slightly saying "May you have peace all the days of your life." The words shocked her as she said them. This form of speech had become outlawed several years ago and she was hit by her school's headmaster for accidently using them a year ago. She never understood why things became outlawed in her country. But she accepted each unexplained change to custom without protest.

The girl continued "My name is Jaeyin, thank you for helping me find a way to escape from those dog beasts of the Pon. They, the trutorjin, had been tracking me for a while after I ventured away from my city into a forbidden area. We are not allowed to wander beyond the sight of the Town-Guardians without permission. I felt adventurous when I came close to the area so I entered it; very foolish on my part."

Her sentences were spoken in a deliberate fashion as if to measure the weight of each word. Simon was amazed that he could understand her fully. He had not yet met a native able to communicate in any European language.

"How has it come to be that you speak my language?" inquired Simon.

"I can begin to explain to you all that you want to know. But I think that," she said while slowing down her rate of speech and lowering her voice "We should continue moving. I do not know if we are out of danger yet."

As they walked, she spoke a few words softly in her native language of Pok Chosun. She had the habit of talking to herself to stay calm. She had known much fear recently in her life; at least the parts she still remembers. She blocked bad memories from her mind because it was the only way she knew in which to cope. In this way she could approach each day with enough energy to do the tasks required by her community to survive.

They followed the path as it moved higher. The clouds soon began to cover their way making it difficult to see. Jaeyin felt more comfortable and at ease in the presence of this one stranger than with the people she had known her whole life. For the first time, she did not harbor distressing feelings of mistrust and caution to anyone not a member of her family. Normally, she considered her words and kept her emotion in check. Among her people, Jaeyin feared that even a word said in jest would destroy her life if it offended some person or precept of her country. She knew that even her two loving parents could not protect her if forces outside the family became upset with her.

Simon sat down next to her and offered her one of two sweetened rice cakes from his pack. They were part of the gifts the local people had given the crew, over a day ago, on the roadside before they made their detour through the mountains.

He placed one cake in her hand. She held it as if considering its value and weight. She looked at Simon as he ate his piece. Satisfied that is was safe Jaeyin took a bite.

As she bit into it Jaeyin felt the emptiness in her stomach. The morsel of food caused a weird sensation to occur. It was the delight of her taste bud as it tasted sweetness. A thing her body recalled from long ago but her brain could not.

After they had finished eating the treat Simon repeated the question "Why do you speak my language? You must tell me how this is possible."

Jaeyin replied "My father used to work up north as an adviser. He was a very learned person who had traveled and studied abroad because my grandfather had been a powerful general. My father managed to study Russian and English as a youth. He then rose in title because of his studious behavior and dedication to work."

"At the beginning of his career he married my mother. Then, after I was born, the fortune of our family changed. First, our grandfather died in mysterious circumstances when I was only three. We lost his protective influence over us. My father suddenly found himself within the wrong group of people in the government which fell out of favor with the ruler Cho Hun, the great grandson of Pon Cho Hut."

"My father is a kind man and spent all his free time teaching me. He was a brilliant instructor of language and I was able to learn a lot in a few short years."

Jaeyin paused for a few moments, thinking about the words she spoke. She did not realize she could speak so eloquently. The pain in her life had left her mostly mute; only speaking when spoken to and never of anything important. She lived behind a protective wall her mind had built which left her incapable of expressing her innermost feeling. At times she felt as if she was the living dead; unable to feel, unable to be creative, unable to love.

Once that pain was allowed to surface and become expressed her mind began to reconnect with her heart; this is how she became eloquent.

She continued her narration "My father was accused of some minor infraction. He was spared execution because of his special skills but we were to be punished. One cannot escape punishment if one behaves differently and does not conform to the dictates of the Pon. We changed residences by force to a simpler one on the outskirts of the great city. My father took to his labor and we, as a family, have lived meagerly since that time over ten years ago."

As they became more relaxed Simon told of his journey around the world. Jaeyin saw the world through his words and became entranced by the images they produced.

Abruptly remembering, Simon reached for something in his pocket. It was the amulet he found when he entered this new land. He took out the handkerchief the amulet was wrapped in. Carefully unfolding it he showed the charmed piece of metal to Jaeyin. "This is what I found when I came into your land. I practically landed on top of it in that pool of water where we met," he explained.

At first, Jaeyin only gazed at the object. Then, and with some hesitation, she touched it. The dark roughness seemed very familiar to her; something close to her life. "This looks like a symbol for our land. I wonder how it arrived at that pool."

Seeing her interest in it, Simon said "Why don't you keep it? I can see you have more affinity for this trinket than I have. Since I found it in your country it probably should belong to one from it." Pausing for a second to consider his thoughts he continued "Yes, I would definitely want you to have it."

"Thank you Simon," she whispered in a soft voice showing how unaccustomed she was to receiving gifts. "I will carry it in my pocket for now." Seconds later she realized her voice was too soft. She changed her tone to one a little harder. "We have been talking awhile without, I am afraid, looking for the way back to my home. But, we must go now before it becomes dark. I think my father will enjoy meeting you."

Simon tried to descend down the path but a force kept him at bay. "Something is happening; I cannot walk any further with you." His physical form began became transparent. Jaeyin reached out to him and grab his hand. It slipped right through it. Simon said to her "I think having that amulet in my possession kept me in your world. But now that I have given it to you I cannot stay. I am slipping away. But, please don't forget me," he said just before he completely disappeared.

She had taken out the amulet from her pocket and tried to hand it back to him; hoping that he would stop fading. But it was too late as he could not grasp anything but instead was completely gone. She said to the air from where he had been "I will never forget you, Simon. I will always remember the joy our conversation has given me."

CHAPTER TWELVE

Jaeyin stood alone stunned by Simon's disappearance. She stared at the space on the ground where he had stood. There, Jaeyin stayed frozen and dazed as her mind tried to reconcile what she had seen. Something, deep in her subconscious, nudged at her and told her to move. This nudge became an inner alert telling her it's time to go.

Jaeyin finally move from her frozen position and began to breathe deeply and regain control of her senses. As she stretched her arms upward, Jaeyin heard footsteps approach. Someone was walking hurriedly toward her. Her heart began to pump harder as this unknown threat came nearer.

Jaeyin ran off the trail and onto loose and unstable shale. It crumbled under the weight of her body. Unable to gain any proper balance, she fell to her left and rolled two meters down. As she tried to stand four guards, of the Ruler surrounded her.

Each guard was dressed in black and wore dark reddish helmets. One guard had his lance lowered, pricking Jaeyin's right shoulder with its tip. She winced as it cut her through the fabric of her clothing. Blood dripped down her arm from the small laceration. Droplets passed under her garment's sleeve and became visible on her hand. She reached over to her shoulder and put some pressure on the wound.

The guard appeared savage, almost wild. He had joined the service of the Pon guards so he could satisfy his craving for torture. Had it not been for the strict orders he received from his superior, he might have done something terrible to Jaeyin.

The Captain of the guards approached. As he was a few decades older than the rest of the guards he moved with heaviness in his legs because his body had become arthritic after many years of service. Nonetheless, his demeanor was that of complete seriousness and control, a quality that had granted him his rank and station.

The Captain barked to the guards "Be careful! The orders have been specific, and I see you may have exceeded them." Upon hearing these words, the guard immediately pulled his lance away from Jaeyin and reached down to lifter her up with powerful arm.

"Yes, Captain. We have delivered the girl as requested."

The senior officer wore a blackish robe with red trim. He walked authoritatively over to Jaeyin and inspected her wound. The captain glared at the guard, who caused Jaeyin to bleed, indicating that any further insubordination would be dealt with harshly.

The captain turned his left and spoke to another guard "You are in charge of prisoner now. Secure her and be certain that she is neither hurt nor does escape. When we get back to the fortress, I want her injury taken care of. Is that understood?"

"Yes, captain!" he replied.

The Captain turned his focus on Jaeyin and said "You are under arrest for defiance of the laws of conduct and propriety set down of our esteemed ruler, the Great Pon Cho Hun. I advise you not to resist your arrest or your punishment will be worse."

Turning and walking back to the path, the Captain kicked the lance of the offending guard, in which he was holding in an improper position with its point touching the ground. The lance flew out of the guard's hand and hit some rocks close by.

The officer waited until the entire squad and Jaeyin were back on the trail. He ordered her shackled and tethered. When completed the captain starting leading them down the trail. Two guards walked right behind her with the rest of the column following closely behind. They kept to the pace of the older officer and did not break this formation until they passed the fortress gates.

As they walked along the day became brighter and brighter and the barren valley became clearer to view. During the march, Jaeyin she tripped over a rock and fell. One guard behind quickly lifted her up without missing a step in the formation."

Each tug of the tether caused her great discomfort due to the tightness of the bindings. Soot and dirt covered her from head to toe. By the time they arrived at the fortress castle seated at the center of the valley she was completely exhausted.

The Captain ordered the guards to clean her up as they entered the square inside the gate.

"After she is clean, bring her below to Tower Three," he added before walking away.

One of the guards walked with her to the nearby well and picked up a bucket off the ground. Another guard undid her bindings. She almost fainted from the release as blood freely pulsed through her arms. Her arms felt tingly as they woke up.

The guard lowered the bucket into the well with a rope that was flung over a bar raised up a half meter from the opening. He filled it with water and then soaked Jaeyin with its cold contents. The guard repeated this whole process until she was shivering in the cool air.

He then forced her to her feet and marched her to a large wooden door. Another guard from the march joined them and pushed the door open. They walked inside, with Jaeyin walking between them. In the opening sat the tower attendant. The guard announced to him "New prisoner being delivered to Tower Three dungeon." The attendant simply responded with an "Okay, proceed."

The three followed a long tunnel to a metal gate. The guard in front told the gatekeeper "Take this prisoner and make her as presentable as possible. She is to be presented to the Chief Magistrate for questioning and sentencing. Also, she will need her injuries attended to."

The keeper motioned to his assistant to escort Jaeyin. The assistant grabbed her wrists and put on lighter metal restraints than she had worn before. Nonetheless, she winced because the metal put pressure on her blistering wrists. He escorted her to a cell where she stood motionless. Moments later two women came into the cell with towels to dry her wet and weary body. As she felt the softness of their touch she fainted. The two women caught her and placed her down on some straw that was on the floor of the cell.

Half an hour later the girl regained consciousness and found herself all alone. She tried to focus on her surroundings but it found it difficult because her cell was faintly lit by a light coming through the cell door. Getting into a sitting position, Jaeyin felt the touch of the amulet against her body from the inside pocket of her shirt.

When she was first caught, her captors first shackled her to prevent her escape. Afterward, they searched her for personal effects. It was because the shackle chains went around her waist that they were unable to detect the amulet in her inside pocket.

Jaeyin was glad to have the amulet. It gave her a sense of calm. She felt it kept her connected to that strange light-haired boy and these thoughts provided her with hope. Her mind wandered briefly as she wondered where Simon had come from and how they had managed to meet in such a strange place.

But her thoughts were cut short when the cell door flew open and two court attendants entered. They lifted her from the floor and put a tether on her restraints. These attendants were different from the Pon guards. They did not carry lances or swords. Instead, they had clubs on their belts to use for managing prisoners.

These court attendants did the bidding of the Magistrate. They acted as bodyguards, servants, and managed courtroom protocol. Because they were not under the direct control of Cho Hun or his generals, they were not allowed more dangerous weapons. This measure prevented the judges from assuming more authority than was required for their positions.

One attendant took the club from his belt and prodded her to move by poking her lower back. The clubs were not for killing but instead for controlling prisoner by inflicting pain with their pointed tips. Jaeyin walked along the corridor with the two following in single file. Repeatedly, the same attendant jabbed her, sending harsh pain up her spine.

The other attendant said "Best you stop that," to the more aggressive one. "The prisoner will not be presentable when called for if you continue. I don't want to have a problem with the Magistrate. That's the last thing you or I need."

After they walked up some stairs and through a corridor the less aggressive attendant stepped out in front of Jaeyin and released the rope from which she was tethered. He forced her into a courtroom where other prisoners were shackled together. They added her to this human chain.

Then, the Magistrate dressed in an impeccable grayish robe entered the court. He was a sharp contrast to the prisoners who reeked of foul odors and had their clothing soiled and torn.

A bailiff called for silence. This was not necessary as the appearance of the Magistrate had a silencing effect on the entire audience in the chamber.

The bailiff continued "His honor, the Chief Magistrate Lee Yi, defender of the Ruler, and protector of the land has entered the chamber."

The Chief Magistrate walked up to a raised platform to sit in his chair. Jaeyin and the other prisoners were lined up on wall to the side of the platform.

The Magistrate sat down and took several parchments from a bailiff. After a few minutes of reading the assorted charges he looked up and asked Jaeyin to be brought forward first and placed in front of the platform alone.

When she was released and in position the Magistrate addressed her "Young lady, I see that you are charged with various acts of sedition; crimes against the most revered Pon Cho Hun and the people of *Bun Dan*. I sentence you for your crime of high treason that you be thrown into the Pit of Treachery, where you will meet your end. In three nights hence this order is to be carried out."

The Magistrate turned to the Bailiff and said "Return this prisoner to her cell making sure she receives one meal per day. We want her to show some energy for the Ruler's prized trutorjin."

The trutorjin were terrible beasts created long ago by sorcery of the founding ruler, Pon Cho Hut. He had a large containment pit built under the fortress castle, where the beasts were tortured to make them terribly ravenous. To stop the trutorjin from digging their way out, a special spell was cast onto the metal barbs that were placed on the walls and ceiling of the containment pit. Not even the ferocity of the beast could make them penetrate the barbs.

These beasts received special training. After days of starvation they were fed live pigs or calves, to enhance their desire for live food. They repeated this method just before prisoner sentencing became carried out.

Jaeyin understood the gravity of her sentence as she had heard tales but she herself had never witnessed fierce beast and its fierce nature. She solemnly walked back to her cell and prayed for a quick death to escape such horror.

That evening three other prisoners were brought to her cell. The court wanted a grander spectacle than just one small girl. Included were a shepherd, an old woman, and a blacksmith. All were charged with sedition to the realm by making unwanted remarks against the laws or traditions of his Divine Ruler, Pon Cho Hun. The neighboring cell had additional prisoners put in them to be ready on the day of carrying out their sentences.

Though the prisoners in Jaeyin's cell were very close together they did not speak even in whisper. They knew that if they were heard saying the wrong words, the attendant would report them and they would receive additional torture.

That was something they did not want to risk. Instead, they just sat down waited for their hour of punishment.

CHAPTER THIRTEEN

Continuing up the path Simon's breathing became heavy and labored. Thin air entered his lungs. He maintained a quick walking pace even as he endured physical discomfort from the altitude.

Sweat, dripping into his eyes, blurred his vision. The blurriness made it difficult for him to see the appearance of a strange object ahead on the trail.

Simon stopped and brushed away the moisture from his eyes with the right sleeve of his shirt. Slowly, focus came back to his vision. What he saw was difficult to comprehend. He stared at it as if waiting for a signal to register in his brain, or something to show that the way was safe to pass.

It seemed that the path trailed off into the open air. That was not entirely accurate. The trail changed to white stone pillars which trailed off into midair. These pillars were a foot apart and stretched no longer than a half meter wide. They appeared as steps slowly going up and out into an abyss. A hundred meters farther out, the pillars became concealed in the mist and Simon could not see where they led.

Simon saw the first pillar was no more than a few centimeters high and perfectly lodged into the mountainside. He jumped upon it to determine its sturdiness. It did not budge under his weight.

He looked over the pillar's edge and saw that the length of the subsequent pillar was longer below and a higher above than the one he stood upon. Simon jumped onto it. It held just the same as the first one.

This time Simon stepped up to the third pillar with more caution because it was further out. It held his footing the same as the previous two. He stopped; looked down and placed one foot on the fourth one, pushing down to see if it would move. It too seemed to be steadfast and firm.

Simon touched it a couple of times more until he was confident the pillar would hold his weight. He felt some moisture on the nape of his neck which made him turn around to see a thick fog moving toward him, obscuring the way he came.

As he turned back to the pillared path, the fog began covered him and the pillars close by. Realizing the dangerous situation that was unfolding, he hurriedly took a step on onto the next pillar and then another. Doing this a few more times Simon stopped.

Looking back he saw the mountain and pillars had become completely shrouded by the fog. The wind now whipped around him with great intensity. Suddenly, a new noise filled his ears beside that of the wind.

He looked back to see the pillars knocking into each other and then falling apart into the abyss. The last pillar he touched crashed into the one where he now stood and started to give way. Simon quickly stepped up onto the next one. The pillar he had just abandoned crumbled and fell. Without further hesitation, he started running faster while anticipating with his eyes which pillar he next would leap onto.

Simon's heart pounded heavily and adrenaline pumped quickly through his body. He pushed himself very had and even though his pace was fast the crumbling pillars stayed perilously footsteps behind.

Simon tripped and fell forward off a pillar. He fell into a patch dense fog where he could barely see his hands. He extended his arms upward and grabbed something that seemed large and steady. He slowly pulled himself up to safety on what appeared to be a large white marble platform. The fog rolled quickly over him and disappeared in the distance. Simon looked out from where he came and did not see any signs of the pillars or their remnants.

A distant golden light filled the far side of the tunnel which led into a mountainside. At its entrance sat two gray stone dragons facing each other. The dragons were four meters high and had fumes bellowing out of their nostrils and mouths. Their tails faced Simon and were opened at their ends. When the wind hit the back of the boy, fire also came out of the dragon's orifices. Simon determined that this happened because wind ran into the tails, became compressed, and fanned the fire sources that existed inside both dragons.

The heat of the fire singed the boy's hair and clothes. When the gust of wind died down, the fire retreated inside the dragons. Simon took this as a cue to run under the heads of the two dragons and into the tunnel entrance.

He felt the intense heat in the belly of both dragons as he passed next to them. Inside the tunnel it was much cooler. Now feeling much calmer Simon walked toward the golden light. He reached the tunnel's end and took one step outside to see a green world full of plant life and trees. The golden light came from the sun that was setting on the horizon.

He walked downward on the mountain slope and came to a place he thought would be good to rest. He sat on some grass and looked at the valley below. It consisted mainly of farms and pastures.

As night fell, he saw the lights of lanterns or stoves come from the houses on each farm. Simon decided to go to the tree line below before it was too dark to move. The boy soon came upon a red pine tree and sat down. There he made a mound of fallen pines for a pillow and went to sleep.

He slept very soundly, mostly because he was exhausted. Not until he heard the first rooster of the morning did his body stir waking him up to begin the day. The pleasing sound of birds chirping lifted his spirits. He followed a path down and took notice of the richness in the landscape. He smelled the fertile ground and yellow wild flowers that filled the meadows as he passed through them.

Simon followed a dirt path to a small house sitting in the middle of several rice paddies. Walking a high berm between the rice paddies, the boy saw the reflection of the sky in the waters below. At the end of the berm sat a small footbridge that Simon needed to cross in order to reach the small farm house.

The house had a garden to its side and a few high leafy trees behind it. He saw somebody working in a vegetable garden removing weeds and hand-watering plants. As he got closer, Simon saw a tall farmer, with a wide brimmed hat wipe the perspiration from his brow as he worked. Crickets beat their wings loudly in the tall reeds near the house.

Walking closer the boy saw a bird cage hanging near the house's entryway with a bird chirping rhythmically to the sound of the crickets. Simon realized that this was the first time he heard these insects since arriving in this strange country.

The sound around the farm triggered a memory in the boy. He remembered a time when he had set sail with his father to South America a few years ago. Before their departure, his father had made a trip from Plymouth to London to attend some government meeting. His father had stopped at a famous confectionery shop before returning home to buy some sweets as a surprise for the long ocean voyage.

On the second day of the voyage his father presented the large box of chocolates he bought to Simon and told him to select one of them. Each day, at the same afternoon hour, his father repeated this offering. Thoughts of the box of chocolates managed to distract Simon for the morning leading up to the daily selection. Only the afternoons were harder for Simon to bear as he read all day from his study books. The drudgery of those afternoons was broken when they finally made landfall in Brazil two months later.

What he recalled when they first came ashore was the sound of crickets. Simons remembers how happy he was when was at his father's side exploring the new town. Since then, crickets have always reminded him of the happy times he has spent with his father.

Simon was about to continue in his reverie of memories when the farmer, owner of the small house, came up to the boy to introduce himself. The farmer's loud voice woke the boy by saying "Son, what are you doing here all alone?"

Simon looked up at the man and responded "I am lost, sir. I have become separated from my friends and hope to find them again somehow."

"Well, come inside," said the farmer. He turned around and walked up to the entryway and pulled the curtain that covered the entrance, signaling for Simon to pass. Simon obliged him by entering the house. The farmer came in and said "You can join my wife and me for lunch," he said pointing to a small table.

The farmer's wife came forward, smiled and bowed to Simon. He saw the kindness in her eyes behind the wrinkles and the lines that old age bestows on the faces of people who have seen many years.

The three sat and ate in silence. As they finished eating, the farmer said "Son we have a small hut outside that you could use to sleep tonight. It is a simple but comfortable thing. Normally, it is used for the drying and storing of our root vegetables. But you can put some straw inside and make a nice bed."

"Thank you, sir. I will wash up in the stream and then prepare my bed," replied Simon.

Simon gratefully accepted this offer of hospitality. He was thoroughly exhausted and in the need of rest.

As the boy nodded off to sleep images of his journey began to replay in his mind. He saw once more the series of events that led him to this farm. He felt at peace here and strangely, trouble-free for the first time since the shipwreck.

CHAPTER FOURTEEN

Together, Keeyun and Wonjoon wandered through the forest thinking of their fellow campers and how they were managing. Much time had passed since last they had seen them. The two boys felt the absence of their friends in their hearts which caused them some concern.

The forest, in which they walked, had mostly trees of red pine. As the two continued, the pines gradually became sparser and became replaced by thicker oak trees. The farther they walked the larger the oak trees seemed to become. Soon the canopy of these trees fully blocked out the sunlight; making the world beneath the branches and leaves full of shadows.

As the oak trees stretched higher into the sky, their root systems became connected underneath the ground. Their links became so knotted that they protruded upward above the ground.

These intertwined roots were everywhere and the boys could no longer step around them. They swallowed up every section of ground between the trees.

Further along, the forest continued its transformation. The linked roots began to shoot upward and the roots had nowhere to go as they grew. Soon they were a meter high and made twists into varying directions. The boys had to weave and turn constantly to make any headway through the forest. For a few moments they became separated and lost sight of each other. Only by calling out and backtracking did they reunite.

The two boys discussed going back in the direction from which they came. At the mention of returning, a light jumped up to the eyes of Keeyun. It then retreated back out into the distance flickered in one solitary space.

"Look Wonja, see that light over there?" Keeyun said, pointing toward the flickering.

"Do you see it?" repeated Keeyun.

"I do," said Wonjoon.

"The strangest thing just happened," continued Keeyun. "I swear that light came right up to me somehow, and then went to where it is now. Don't know if I am tired or just not seeing correctly."

"Your mind may be playing tricks but one thing is for sure. There is a light there. Must mean someone is camping. Let's follow it and ask to join them," replied Wonjoon.

"I agree that we have no other choice. I don't think any other direction will lead us to anything suitable," said Keeyun.

The boys followed the light and almost reached it when something odd happened. It streaked backward fifty meters or so. Approaching the light one more it again retreated.

"This light means to play with us," said Wonjoon "To taunt us. I don't know if we should be following it."

"I think it may be trying to show us the way in which to go," said Keeyun thinking about it.

No sooner had those words left his mouth than the light stopped moving and its shine grew brighter until it illuminated an entire area directly ahead of the two boys.

Upon seeing the light halt the two boys rushed forward, curiosity overcoming any fear they held to get a look at its' source. As they got closer, an ear-piercing shriek came from behind them making them trip and fall over some tree roots. Next it was the sound of a howl that chilled them to their bones as they lay on the ground. Not waiting for whatever beast was out there, they picked themselves up and ran.

A minute later Keeyun arrived at the edge of the clearing. His eyes took a few seconds to adjust to the brightness of this enclosed area. But before Keeyun could focus, Wonjoon came stumbling into him. Keeyun managed to stay on his feet but Wonjoon fell again to his knees past Keeyun.

Keeyun remained upright and did not move much after Wonjoon hit him. His eyes began to focus on and examine his new surroundings. He saw an old man with a white beard sitting behind a small campfire. This small fire miraculously illuminated the entire field.

Keeyun looked behind him and saw the opening in the clearing from which they had entered begin to close. He pointed at this occurrence so Wonjoon could see it, too.

The boys walked closer to the fire. The bearded man was smaller in stature than both Keeyun and Wonjoon. His body seemed to glow along with the fire. His clothing was very white, well-kept, and perfectly neat.

As the boys approached he stood up and put on a grayish robe which dimmed his glowing body. As he stood the boys could see much better the outline of his face which was perfectly smooth. His eyes were jet black and glinted in the light from the fire. They saw that his skin seemed ageless. Even though even had some youthfulness about him he gave off the impression of being much older.

The man's appearance was a sharp contrast to that of the boys because they looked disheveled in their soiled clothes. They had not taken the time to clean themselves during their entire adventure as they were accustomed to doing at home.

"Welcome young ones. You are safe now from the beasts of the forest. Here in this clearing, nothing comes in that I don't allow," said the old man.

As the boys adjusted to their new surroundings, the old man continued "Time you got here. I was beginning to have my doubts that you'd ever arrive," as he motioned the boys to come closer with his hand.

Wind raced around the trees of the field for a few brief seconds, rustling the fallen brown leaves and branches. The old man sat down. The boys, still standing, became a little mesmerized by the light emanating from his eyes as they approached.

"Look old man," Keeyun spoke with an impatient tone. Agitation and fatigue were making Keeyun act less than his normal respectful self. "I do not know of what you are talking about. But my friend and I are tired, hungry, and lost. What we would like is some food and directions. Do you have any food of which you could share with us?"

Wonjoon sensed that this man was more than an elderly peasant and did not want to displease him. He grabbed Keeyun by the shoulder and motioned that he would do most of the talking.

Wonjoon began "Good sir, we are lost campers who have been separated from our party. What my tired friend is trying to convey is that we are need of some respite from our long travel. We would be most obliged with any assistance you can offer us."

"I have seen you both in my vision and know how you came to be here today," responded the old man. "This is no coincidence indeed. Please take a seat and share in my humble meal and I will explain further."

"Thank you kind sir," said Wonjoon, truly grateful.

Wonjoon chose the log to the right and was the first to sit down. He felt the warmth come from this simple fire. It elevated his spirits. Wonjoon motioned to Keeyun to sit down likewise.

Keeyun was a little more hesitant than Wonjoon. But after a few seconds he too sat upon a log placed to the left of Wonjoon.

When Keeyun seated himself Wonjoon said "I want to say that you should forgive my friend's hasty words. Our journey has been long and harsh. Harshness like this can ruin the manners of even a very decent person."

"Hmm," responded the old man "Is it possible that so many years of good manners could be so easily lost, especially here while sitting next to an inviting fire under this beautiful night?"

On mention of that Wonjoon looked up at the sky, which was remarkably filled with more stars than he ever remembered seeing before. Keeyun did not stare up as Wonjoon but kept looking at the old man, vigilantly.

The old man allowed Wonjoon a few more seconds to look at the night sky and then said "You two move your logs closer to the fire and share in of my humble meal of rice and roots. I hope these simple staples will be enough for you both. As a monk I cannot offer you what you are accustomed to eating at your homes."

The elderly man picked up four chopsticks and gave two to each boy to eat. Then he used a small bowl to scoop out rice and vegetables from the pot into two larger wooden bowls and handed them to Keeyun and Wonjoon.

They two boys ate hastily as the feeling of hunger overwhelmed any sense of propriety. Wonjoon noticed that their host ate much slower and he felt slightly embarrassed. He tapped his bowl so Keeyun would look up. Wonjoon said "Let's try and show some manners to our host while we eat." Keeyun nodded yes in reply and took a deep breath and smiled at the monk to show his gratitude for his hospitality and food. The old man smiled back at Keeyun in understanding.

The old man did not say a word until the boys had eaten their fill. Finally with the boys fed and somewhat rested he began to speak "My sons, I am but a humble monk who has wandered through the forest and mountains of our land for many years. I have mostly kept to myself. At times I have bartered with peasants for food or clothing.

The monk continued "Once, a long time ago, I lived a very different life. I was a prosperous merchant living in the capital city. But tragedy struck my family. The lives of my wife and two daughters were lost when a mob became enraged for some injustice that regularly besets the common man. My dear loved ones were walking near the royal palace when they were trapped between palace guards and an enraged mob. A skirmish ensued and they were trampled."

"From that moment on, the image of the world in my mind became shattered and I knew only despair. I could not carry on any further with my merchant business since the reason for it had faded. With my ambitions and desire gone I closed up my shop and retired. I spent many weeks sitting in in my room above the shop venturing outside only a few times to buy some food."

The monk took a deep breath and continued "Then one day I decided to make a donation of all my belongings. I opened my doors and gave everything away to whoever came by. It seemed like a festival as I gladly gave to neighbors and strangers the belongings earned over my life. Next, I had my property and business sold. I gave it to a young couple for a fair price so they could start to have a good life and begin a family. I donated a part of the sale to a local temple. The rest I kept to use later."

"I left the city and searched out a way to soothe the hurt lodged so deep in my heart. In the wilderness, I took to meditation in hope that I could alleviate my suffering. I prayed a lot and walked without much sleep for weeks in the mountains. My body endured much but the pain I felt was in the heart."

"When I slept I saw my family and then the tragedy repeated itself. I found it difficult to think and function while awake. Gaunt and distraught, I began to approach madness. I was ready to relinquish my body up to the heavens and join my family by crossing the hidden dimension that separates us when alas, death did not come," the old monk said solemnly, dropping his voice as memories flooded his mind.

Wonjoon closed his eyes. The images of the story became alive as he saw the monk as a younger man suffering in the city and then in the wilderness. Wonjoon opened his eyes and the images disappeared.

The monk then carried on with his tale "Eventually my sanity returned. I think because I was in a weak state of mind I began to make excuses for my existence. Not wanting to admit that I was not strong enough to go on living but scared of dying I decided to stop moving and see what fate would hand me."

"So there I sat among the dried leaves of a forgotten autumn waiting for something to happen, waiting for fate itself to take me, when a strange thing happened."

"A young doe, probably born a few days earlier, came upon me as I sat motionless. She walked up next me without fear or mistrust, as that is the gift of youth. She stood in front of and we stared at each other. I felt as if I was swimming in its' eyes which were big and dark brown. We continued this staring for close to an hour. Then, I felt the pain and sadness leap from my heart and into the sky above. It was the compassion I received that allowed me a small sampling of hope. That was enough to dash away the heaviness I felt in my heart."

"A short while later the doe walked away and I forced myself upright. Right there for reasons unclear to me my sadness became replaced by anger. It filled me as I walked in circles around a tree for hours. I vented a voice of rage into the winds until weariness stopped me."

"When I could take no more I lay down again and went to sleep. There I found my first peaceful sleep since the occurrence of the tragedy.

"The following weeks I meditated on my condition. I imagined that to move forward as a human I would need to learn to become different. I wanted to shatter the image of myself and build a new me. To achieve this new state I needed to concentrate on a new task. I decided to work on farms as a laborer. Soon changes took root in my soul as my heart opened with acts of selfish charity. I continued to meditate and practice selfishness until I was sure my heart was fully changed. As it turned out I became stronger mentally and physically leaving me in the state I am now. Of course there is more to my story but I want you to understand a little for now," and with those final words the monk and remained silent.

The three of them sat quietly for a while. A bird chirping happily broke the silence as it felt the rise of the sun making a new day. As sunlight filled the opening the boys looked around the field and saw the flowers of Sharon in bloom growing in abundance.

The monk, who had been motionless, moved his head from side to side to wake his neck muscles. As he began to speak again the two boys refocused their attention on him.

"As my ability to meditate became stronger I sensed subtle changes occurring in the land. I have developed a keen awareness to change; an ability that has led me to see a rising and threatening force that will harm our kingdom. The average man cannot see or feel these changes as they are caught up in their daily pursuits. But I have stepped outside the common life and therefore not indifferent to the greater truths around us."

"What I have to tell you two is that these changes are insidiously entering our kingdom and will alter our lives permanently if something is not done to stop them. It feeds off our blindness and ignorance. It grows stronger daily as the common man feels falsely secure. Our indifference is now fueling it and will bring an end to our peaceful way of life."

Wonjoon was perplexed by these remarks. He had not seen any suffering in his village and had not heard of any in the kingdom. But he did take into account the recent strange events that happened to them.

The monk saw the light of recognition in the young Wonjoon.

"The people are living in a happy delusion. They fill their free time with meaningless games and frivolity. They do this to counter the fear they feel in their hearts. Many sense these changes but refuse to examine and understand them. They prefer to live like turtles in a shell; hidden from the true reality."

"But these changes will come, nonetheless; that I promise you," the old monk sternly said to the boys.

The monk took a pause as if to let the early morning breeze make his words seem lighter.

"It has been almost five years that I felt this threat. I have preached in village squares and have talked to many elected officials. But no one is willing to listen. They do not trust the ramblings of an old monk," he said.

"For five years I have extended my senses to see the root of this new wickedness and the mystery that lies beneath. There existed a leader over two centuries ago whose younger brother became fascinated by the dark forces found in obscure regions around the world. His name was known as Pon Cho Hut. Born with physical defects in his heart he sought to strengthen his constitution through any means possible. He was persuaded by the mysteries of the occult that it would heal him. As his mind became more and more perverted he became swayed by the idea of carving a dark kingdom out of the ancient land of *Ilhanung*."

"He learned to use the trait of indifference and the fear of the common citizenry to his advantage. He began to take small parcels of land through the use of black magic. He obtained more and more portions until half the land became veiled behind darkness. He summoned an energy he did not clearly understand. In this energy he set in motion a darkness that will soon consume our land and beyond."

"Right now the sick, the weak, and the invalid of our land are aiding this force. This is why I stumbled upon the truth. In my meditation, I came to realize that I was feeling the dark grown force and it in turn blackened my heart. Only by miracle was I saved from despair. The doe either by accident or by design freed my soul and allowed me to see much more deeply with my heart. I developed clairvoyant powers that guide me in understanding the changing world around us."

These thoughts seemed too complex for the boys. But they still managed to follow the story as the monk continued "These negative energies are rising and the positive energy of people becomes diminished. This dark shadow will grow unless someone or something stops its advance. I believe it must be the collective will of the people. Only their spiritual energy can reject the shroud that will soon befall us all."

The boys were overwhelmed with those final words. Keeyun got up to his feet and shouted "Enough of such dark stories. I have heard enough of things like this around campfires and school grounds to last me a lifetime."

Wonjoon reacted differently. He stood up a little shakily and walked over to Keeyun to comfort him.

"Calm yourself, my friend," said Wonjoon even though he too felt the same unease in his heart. He wondered about the validity of the old man's words; not really wanting to accept them.

Abruptly, Keeyun raised his voice and said "Let us go now."

"I agree," replied Wonjoon "I don't want to stay either."

While dark thoughts rose in their minds, the two boys tried to find a way out of the clearing. They felt fear begin to choke them and becoming feverish, they desperately searched for an exit. The trees seemed to spin around the clearing making it unbearable. Unable to resist the effect of dizziness, they fell to the ground, unconscious.

CHAPTER FIFTEEN

Drizzling rain woke the boys up. The sky was dark as evening had set. The boys found themselves in bedrolls near the fire that now was only smoldering ash. They somehow slept in bedrolls near the burnt out fire the monk had set. The monk was nowhere to be seen. A harsh wind from the approaching storm entered the opening. The boys climbed out of their bedrolls and scanned the area.

"Kee, let's take these bedrolls with us. They will serve us well for the next time we camp," said Wonjoon.

"That's a good idea Wonja," responded Keeyun as he stretched out his arms above his head to loosen up. Then, the boys crossed the field and found a path leading out; a path that had escaped their view earlier.

"Wonder why we were unable to see this before?" asked Keeyun.

"I don't know. Maybe the monk weaved some spell that kept us blind. But one thing is for certain I don't like the tricks he pulls," answered Wonjoon. "I don't like it at all. And I certainly don't think we can trust him."

They found a wider pathway without the problems they had earlier encountered leading up to the opening. After walking for a while the winds picked up and ripped along the trail. The trees funneled the wind quickly down the pathway. The boys picked up their pace as the weather seemed to turn for the worse.

Keeyun expressed his concern "Wonja, we should be looking for some shelter. My body feels chilled," he said as a cold sensation invaded his body making him feel severely uncomfortable.

Wonjoon felt the cold too but was better able to resist it. He saw his friend start to shiver and began to worry. "I know Kee, it's bad, but I don't know where we can find some. Let's just continue on in this direction. Keeping our bodies moving will help fend off the cold, at least till we come upon somewhere to keep us safe from these conditions," said Wonjoon.

Then the rain started again and the air temperature fell making the situation worse. Soon the wetness on the ground turned to a film of ice making it difficult for Keeyun and Wonjoon to keep their balance standing.

"I have an idea," called out Wonjoon to his friend over the sound of the wind. "Let's tie a cloth around our feet with some small stones on the bottom. That should help us keep our footing as we walk."

Wonjoon cut some strips from their bedroll as Keeyun dug up some pebbles with a large stone. They wrapped the pebbles between the cloth and the soles of their sandals. It proved to a good improvement because they had more traction for walking and additional warmth from the fabric.

As the weather turned colder Keeyun began chattering uncontrollably. His hands and feet started to turn blue as his core body temperature dropped.

Wonjoon sensed that Keeyun's condition was quickly becoming life threatening. He yelled to his friend "Kee, run! We must run to stay warm."

They both moved their legs as fast as they could. But the slippery ice thwarted their efforts at moving quickly, making it difficult to warm up their bodies.

Eventually, they made it to a dip in the trail and rolled down into a small gorge below where the wind was weaker. As they made their way through the gorge they noticed that the rain did not fall there. Coming to the end of the gorge they emerged into a clearing where they felt the touch of warm air on their faces. It seemed as if they had leapt back into summer. Keeyun's condition immediately started to improve and color returned to his whitened face. Within a few minutes his body returned to normal with no visible aftereffects.

As Keeyun recovered Wonjoon examined the place to which they arrived. The clearing was a small circle about forty paces across. To his surprise the monk materialized in front of him at the center of the area in some kind of trance-like state.

Wonjoon walked up to the monk to greet him. He saw the old man had his legs and arms folded and his body seemed somehow suspended a few centimeters off the ground.

Wonjoon curiously reached out to touch the monk when he came out of his trance and extended his legs to stand erect. Keeyun feeling much better approached and saw the monk wake up.

"May your day be peaceful, my young friends," said the old man. "I hope you were able to find some rest during the night."

He continued "I am glad that we are together once again. Now I can continue to explain the deep purpose of our meeting together during these troublesome times." He motioned the boys to take up seats near him; as they did the previous day.

Keeyun wanted to express the agitation he felt about the monk's behavior. But he held his tongue and sat down.

"My young fellow, I want to tell you of an amulet that was forged by an order of Xingjian monks who lived long ago in faraway snowcapped mountains to the west. In one special mountain lied their perched monastery where the pious monks dedicated themselves to two pursuits, meditation and making of protective metal adornments. They became highly renowned for their magical trinkets. Many nobles of nearby lands journeyed up to the monastery to obtain them. The nobles always offered payment in gold or silver but the monks only accepted promises of living spiritual lives as the only form of payment."

"One day the head monk, chosen for his station because of his wisdom, had a vision. In it he saw a great danger that would soon arise on the planet, a danger so perverse and terrible that it would alter time itself and destroy the delicate balance of harmony in nature that allowed for happiness to exist."

"He decided to make have his hundred or so monks make an extraordinary effort, to make a talisman, an amulet that would have tremendous power in subduing dark magic. He knew the task would be arduous and difficult for his monks; a point of such difficulty that each resident of the monastery may lose their lives in the combined effort of making it. Even with such a high risk the head monk commanded the others to begin the work regardless to the sacrifice."

"They smelted the talisman from ancient metals discovered deep in the bowels of their mountain. They worked for over a month in shifts performing a repeated folding while others chanted in an ancient language until the amulet possessed the very power of creation. Inside it they stored a portion of the original essence of the universe where life began."

"Many of the monks died at the exhaustive nature of this task. Their souls became added to the amulet's power and reside in it still."

"Each willingly gave his life for creating something to help a troubled future; a future of people they would never come to know; a truly unselfish act."

"As the process of making the amulet came to an end most of the monks with the exception one passed away under the duress of the task."

In the clearing the old monk had stood the whole time telling of the story. Suddenly, a look of weariness came across his face and he sat down. Wonjoon saw his loss of energy and immediately stood up to offer assistance. The old man waved at him that he needed no help. Instead he said "Sit, too, my young friend. Please forgive me that telling of tale has taken away my energy. It is not an easy story remember and tell correctly."

When they were all seated the old monk continued "This last monk took the amulet which was still extremely hot out of the forge and placed it on window ledge for it to cool. The monk was exhausted and did not realize his error at the time but the newly instilled power left the amulet unstable and very light. The amulet flew away in a cool breeze out the window and fell a thousand meters. It continued to cool as it fell and then was lifted up and taken away by a powerful gust of wind. It sailed through the air and then fell on some large rocks of the creek bed far from the monastery."

The monk continued his explanation "The prophecy told the monks to leave a small fissure in the center of the amulet. I believe this fissure was left so that it would be deliberately broken. When it fell it separated into two pieces along its fissure. The inner piece was formed in the shape of a teardrop while the other its' outline."

"The one shaped like a teardrop bounced away from the boulder into a stream flowing under the rocks. The other stayed on the boulder in clear sight."

"The last remaining Xingjian monks searched for the amulet. He came upon the outer outline form lying on a boulder. See the inner piece missing he continued his search. It proved impossible because the other piece had floated away in the brook below into a crack in the Earth."

"The story almost ends here, a tragic tale. Because the magic of reconciliation was not wielded and many wars and civil strife took place that it could have prevented. Now we come to the crucial point in time when a force beyond our reckoning threatens us. Neither do we have the amulet or our sense of time in history. We forget our beginnings which will help add to our destruction. We cannot change people hence we must rely on the joining of the amulet to keep us protected until it is learned how to combat the dark forces of the planet without assistance. The amulet if joined would start the process of opening the minds of the people and relieve us of this shroud that covers us."

The boys stood up and walked around to talk privately. Keeyun talked in a whispered voice "These tales are no more than puffs of smoke. I don't believe them. I have never seen this fear he talks of in our village."

"I don't know what to believe, Kee," responded Wonjoon. "I wish we were home and this was just some dream. But I feel that it is not and there may be some truth in his words. Let's keep our wits about us and see if he can help us find our way home."

The monk drank water from a small flask as he waited for them to rejoin him.

As the boys approached, the monk turned to them and raised his hand saying "Before you make any requests please let me finish my story. It is almost over."

"Do so quickly, sir!" said Wonjoon. "We must be on our way."

"Agreed, my young gentleman," replied the old man. "It so happens that we are coming to the end of the tale."

"This ancient monk I talked about became the guardian of the amulet half. He spent his life guarding it whiles all the time searching for other half. The Xingjian monk found a young apprentice who he trained to do the same once he died. This has happened for three centuries.

"One day in my wanderings I came upon an elderly monk. He was distraught at having lost his young follower to some illness. Also, the elderly monk knew he did not have more than a year of his life remaining. He entrusted me with the amulet half and related the same story that I have told you," said the old man as he took the amulet half out of his pocket and showed it the boys.

The old man held it up to Wonjoon. "This is part of the magical talisman that can help render peace to our land. I believe that our meeting here was not by chance. Wonjoon, you will be the last apprentice of the amulet. You will find that this part of the amulet gives its bearer a healthier and longer life than normal. You see I have aged much slower since I received it over forty years ago. Today is my ninety-third birthday."

"Incredible, sir," said Wonjoon. "I would not have believed that you were more than sixty years old."

"This is too much to believe, Wonja," said Keeyun warily. "Are we to believe whatever this stranger tells us?"

The old man responded to Keeyun's accusation "I know you have doubts. But you will see after you accept my portion of the amulet that you will see more clearly and see the division of the ancient *Ilhanung*."

Keeyun continued his protest "We only want to make our way back to our camping party and then, our homes. So be helpful and show us which way we should go."

The old one had a brief expression of anger at the insolence of the youth cross his face. But he let the emotion pass and resume his calm demeanor. He raised his head up and added to the story "It was foretold by our elders that a great division would come upon our land and create havoc and ruin that would spread throughout the world; eventually destroying it and every living creature. To prevent this from happening, these two pieces must be re-joined by those that carry them in the Tajii Chamber and soon."

"This chamber lies somewhere within the point of separation between the two lands. I have come close to finding the way to this chamber after taking possession of my portion of the amulet but to no avail. I feel that the amulet will not allow me to find it because of my past transgressions therefore I feel that you Wonjoon are chosen to take up the amulet half, find its sister and join them together to protect us all."

"Have you ever seen the other half?" asked Wonjoon.

"Yes," responded the monk. "I searched in some underground caves near where it had become lost. I had it momentarily when it slipped into a stream and passed further underground. I believe it rejected me and decided to find someone worthier than I to accomplish the task. I know you can succeed whereby I will know only failure."

"Old man, you talk very mysteriously about chambers and amulets, this and that," responded Wonjoon in a changed tone. "But what of the division are you speaking? I can recall my entire life well and the land has never changed. It has always been whole and under one king."

"That is not the case, though I wish it were," replied the monk.

"Have you not seen strange signs since you were small boys? Your memory is short because of your youth you do remember comments from the elders of the village saying how the darkness grows and strange things are sometimes seen. I tell you that there is a change coming, a momentous change and if we do not do something now to reverse it our lives and way of live will become lost. Profound suffering of everybody will follow, of that I am certain. What was set in motion a long time ago will lead to all our destruction. No one will remain untouched," said the monk.

The old man walked up to Wonjoon and placed the amulet half in his hand. He closed the hand of Wonjoon around it and said "Remember, many have given their lives in servitude to protecting this half, in the hopes of one day establishing true peace. I entrust you to finish the task before it is too late."

The old monk turned and walked to the entrance and picked up a staff sitting near the white roots of a great tree. He turned to the boys and cried out "Remember to accept assistance from anyone or anything that offers, any rejection of help will only help the forces of darkness and your efforts will prove fruitless."

As the old man touched the branch of one tree an opening appeared he stepped through it and disappeared. Seconds later, the opening became larger and the boys found themselves back in the middle of a heavily wooded area.

"What do you think?" Keeyun asked Wonjoon. "This is the strangest of things, meeting this monk and you receiving this trinket, called an amulet."

"I half believe him," said Wonjoon. "I was thinking of how strange things have become. We have this idea about how good are lives are at the moment. What if our small perfect reality stops us from seeing this peril that will infect our community and the whole country? We cannot turn our backs to this threat or everything we know will be lost."

"Also, I remembered what the elders have been saying in whispers at night among themselves. They don't think I paid attention but I did. They talked of relatives and friends who have gone mysteriously missing. I don't want to live with my eyes closed any longer. I want to take action," said Wonjoon.

Wonjoon continued trying to analyze the events of his life leading up to this moment. "I remember many fitful dreams I have had over the year of gloom and darkness. I cannot believe that is normal since we really never had anything bad happen to us or our village. These dreams must have been premonitions to the evil that is coming."

A giant rainbow formed in the distance from the descending sun. They felt good at once as the golden beam of light shined on their faces. As they walked in the direction of the rainbow they began to accept their task and its importance.

When the sun disappeared behind clouds in the sky rain and darkness followed.

"Well," Wonjoon said with a sigh, resigning himself to the worsening weather conditions "Time to get going. We are running out of time. This storm may never let up if we don't act now."

"Right behind you Wonja. I am starting to feel convinced that the old monk was not completely insane. I have thought about our strange circumstance and it could only some evil force behind it. Okay, I am with you now and will do whatever is needed to help you accomplish your task," Keeyun said trying to bolster his spirit.

They trudged along resolutely through some marshy fields as the clouds lowered themselves to their level, limiting their vision to only twenty meters. They trekked the whole day over soaked grounds looking for a road that would lead them north. They were sure of what direction the needed to travel but felt sure it was toward the north.

CHAPTER SIXTEEN

The branches of the trees swayed back and forth as the boys found themselves under a downpour of a frightening storm. Water ran everywhere until the hope of finding a good trail became close to impossible. They walked, looking for any significant landmark to get their bearings. Keeyun climbed a sturdy tree to get a good view of the area. "Wonja, come up here and have a look," he said with a hint of enthusiasm.

"Be right there," Wonjoon said. Just as he walked toward the tree, he felt a sensation in his chest as if his heart had briefly stopped. He doubled over in pain and knelt to the ground.

He used his will to force himself to breathe. As the musty and damp forest air entered his lungs, his heart resumed its normal beating. The pain slowly subsided as he looked upward.

He stood up and walked up to the tree gingerly, not sure what he had just experienced. He put his palm on the tree trunk to steady himself and keep from falling.

Keeyun looked down at his friend and asked "Is everything all right?"

"Yes, I felt terribly ill for a few seconds. But whatever I had, has passed," answered Wonjoon.

"Can you make it up the tree?" asked Keeyun with obvious concern in his voice.

"Yes, just give me a few seconds."

Taking a deep breath Wonjoon began to go up. He climbed slowly and deliberately to make sure he was strong enough. His limbs tingled as blood rushed to his hands and feet. As he moved methodically, his mind wandered to thoughts of his mother. He said a prayer they had recited together many times to ask for strength as he went upward.

Wonjoon made it up to the branch opposite his friend. Keeyun said "I think we have found ourselves in the middle of a large tract of rice paddies. I remember my father telling me how difficult they are to walk through when the rains are plentiful. It will be hard making our way through them." He studied the land some more and then said "Let's try and go along that higher point over there."

Wonjoon nodded in agreement and looked out on the paddies as the rain began to ease up.

"I don't see where there's an end to these paddies," he said jumped down and leaned upon the tree with his back.

Keeyun jumped out in front of Wonjoon. He turned to his friend and said "Wonja, don't get your spirits down. We both want to see our families very much. In order to do that, we need to keep moving or we'll be stuck here forever." He shook Wonjoon's shoulder to give him some assurance.

Wonjoon replied "Of course, you're right. My body is just feeling a bit weak; that is all. I promise to keep up with you so we can get out of here."

They started out in the direction of the ridge that rose among the two paddies. They had to slosh through a great deal of water and wade through mud. They made their way under a nest of a wisp of snipes. The bird's nest rested on a high branch to deter curious squirrels from getting close. But the mother in the nest did not take any chances with the boys as they passed underneath. She gave off menacing sounds to warn them that they were not wanted.

The boys walked slowly along the small ridge as it became higher in elevation by several meters. During the uphill hike, they had to pull their legs out of the mud constantly with their hands. Movement was a real struggle. Ten minutes later they managed to get to the higher ground which was less muddy and easier to travel on.

The ridge ended and the boys descended down to a small stream. As chance would have it, a hollowed-out log rested on its bank. The boys decided to float down the stream on the log instead of walking alongside the stream.

Wonjoon and Keeyun sat in the center of the log and drifted down the stream, thankful that they were no longer sloshing through the mud.

The water became deeper and they made sure not to move about too much to avoid the risk of capsizing. They floated peacefully for a while, covering a good distance due to the fast current.

The stream widened a little and then suddenly dropped two meters. The boys were tossed about but managed to stay on the log. As they looked around they saw they were headed right into a thicket of fallen trees and branches. The water pooled around the trees and made a natural dam.

When they hit a thick branch, the swirling water pushed the log partially down below the surface. As the boys stood slightly upright, as was their instinct, the log began to take on more water. The log overturned throwing the boys into the water. They were pulled under due to a fast current.

Unable to swim, they panicked and started flailing under the water with their arms and legs. At the brink of passing out, two large hands from the surface grabbed Keeyun and pulled him upward. These hands were connected to a strong man. Because of the water in his eyes, Keeyun could not make out who the man was, but felt himself placed safely on a fallen log above the waterline.

By the time the large fellow started searching for Wonjoon in the water, the boy had become unconscious. With his head underwater and his legs wrapped around a branch to give him leverage, the man was able to free Wonjoon from the entanglement. He swung the unconscious boy out of the water and placed him next to Keeyun.

Keeyun leaned over and grabbed his friend's hand. Worriedly, he repeatedly tapped it while calling out his name. Wonjoon did not stir but remained in a lifeless state.

The large man pulled himself up out of the water and came over to Wonjoon. He placed his hand over the mouth and nose of the motionless boy to check his breathing.

Keeyun felt desperate at the prospect of losing his best friend. "Please, we must do something," he pleaded as his eyes moved between Wonjoon and the big man.

Without so much as a word, the large man raised Wonjoon up and dropped him facing down upon his bent knee. Wonjoon's body buckled upward at the impact. Keeyun felt relief at seeing his friend move.

Gasping, Wonjoon spurted out the water which had collected in his lungs. The big man then lifted him up again and placed Wonjoon on his shoulders. The extra weight did not slow him down as he walked with a quickened gait down a pathway that ran near the dam.

Slowly Keeyun stood up, feeling a little shaky from this incident. He proceeded to follow them but found himself already far behind.

"Wait, wait," shouted Keeyun feebly. His plea was heard by no one. Unsure of his whereabouts he continued down the path.

As he walked, he realized he had sprained his right ankle, making movement very painful. He limped down the path until he came to a fallen tree. He broke off a strong branch with the weight of his body. Using the branch as a crutch, he slowly moved down the path.

Trudging along, Keeyun started to wonder if he would ever find them. "I hope that big man doesn't forget me. Maybe he will come back when he sees that I haven't yet caught up with them," he said to himself.

Stopping to look around, he heard what sounded like an animal. Instead, it was the large man. He had come back for him. Keeyun let out a sigh of relief that his ordeal would soon be over.

He waved hello to the man. The large man brushed aside the boy's hand and picked him up like a sack of rice. He flung Keeyun easily over his shoulder and returned the way he came. After only a few minutes they came in sight of a small cabin. As they approached, Keeyun saw smoke rising from a small brick chimney at the back of the dwelling.

The man put the boy foot-first on the ground. Keeyun uttered an inaudible 'thank you'. The large man breezed into the house which seemed too small for his size and stature

Keeyun entered much more cautiously. He walked inside and felt the warmth of a stove fire from the far side of the room. An enticing aroma reached his nostrils. He walked over and sat near the simmering kettle. His stomach felt hollow and ached for the food.

A small woman came up to Keeyun and ladled out a good portion of soup into the bowl she was holding. She grabbed a wooden spoon from the chimney mantel and handed both the bowl and spoon to Keeyun. He tasted one spoonful. It burnt the inside of his mouth but he did not mind. He ate the next couple of spoonsful slowly by letting each one cool before eating. Even with a burnt mouth, he enjoyed the delicious meat and potato stew.

After a few more helpings he realized his friend was sitting nearby. Wonjoon was eating, too. Keeyun felt pleasantly glad for the whole experience. Enjoying the food he remained silent the entire time.

When they finished the farmer spoke up "A very bad day to be out, don't you agree, Oma," addressing the woman who appeared to be his spouse.

"Yes, dear," she responded while turning to address the boys "What brings you out on such a day?" Before getting an answer she added "You know you are very lucky my husband spotted you both. Otherwise the worst might have occurred. But let's be thankful nothing bad happened."

The old woman continued "Anyway, looks like my husband solved two problems tonight; your rescue and the protection of our dam. If you had died there, the bears would have tried to get at you and have ruined our irrigation system. So you can see we are very pleased by the outcome. My husband hates to redo things."

Wonjoon and Keeyun did not know whether or not she was jesting with them. But they were grateful nonetheless and chose to be silent, out of courtesy.

The big man gave them blankets with which they wrapped themselves up snuggly by the fire, all nice and warm.

Wonjoon thought he was dreaming when a golden apparition appeared in the corner of the room. It was a boy not much older than he. Wonjoon sat up mesmerized and stared at the yellow haired boy with blue eyes. Keeyun also sat up as he turned and saw this new person.

The golden haired boy walked toward them. He extended his hand to Wonjoon and said "Hi, my name is Simon. I am pleased to make your acquaintance. I have been sitting quietly in the shadow of the corner waiting for the right time to introduce myself."

Before waiting for an answer, Simon walked over to Keeyun and shook his hand too. "How did you two wind up floating down that creek in the middle of the paddies?" he said with a smile not leaving his lips.

"My name is Wonjoon and my companion here is called Keeyun. Being the rains were very heavy, we became lost. It was difficult to walk so when we came upon this log in a creek, it seemed the logical choice. We didn't expect to get caught on the dam and then sucked underneath. If it was not for our large host we would have perished, and for that we are grateful."

"An interesting tale, indeed," Simon said as he continued to smile.

"Let me tell you about myself. I come from a place many leagues across the great water and have arrived recently in your country because the ship I was traveling on was lost at sea."

"As for our kind mutual host, his name is Bae and the name of his sweet wife is Chuna. He also rescued me but not in such a dramatic fashion as you two. He took me in and gave me shelter after I had become separated from my traveling party."

Wonjoon stood up and turned to face Simon. The curiosity of his golden hair was too much to resist. He took a step closer to touch the hair. It seemed almost as warm as the fire.

Simon allowed the brief touch because he knew his hair was a curiosity to them. After a few seconds, he walked over and took a seat by the fire. Remembering his manners, Wonjoon walked over to Bae and bowed, then gave his thanks. Wonjoon signaled to Keeyun to stand up and do the same.

Bae greeted them both with a solemn face; a face that had seen many years which tempered his emotions. Nevertheless, his advanced age did not leave him feeble. He was a massive individual, the largest person Wonjoon had ever seen.

Bae handed both boys small cups of hot tea. The warmth of its contents felt delightful. They took their cups and returned to their places near the fire.

The activity in the house became still and no one spoke. The silence lingered until it reached an awkward state. Since Keeyun was not one for holding his tongue for too long, he was the first to speak "We all come from the land of *Hana*. But you Simon do not. How does such a stranger come from such a distant land and then, find himself on this particular farm in our kingdom?"

Eager to answer, Simon said "I was on an ocean voyage to go see my father on an island far to the south of your land. During the voyage, we ran into a terrible storm and I, along the crew, became shipwrecked on an island off the coast of Hana. My companions and I took a boat from the island to here in search of passage to continue sailing south. Some bad luck befell our party and I became separated from them. These kind people took me in and have since taken care of me. I can tell you that your land *Hana* is quite strange, almost surreal. It feels as if it is constantly changing before me. When I think I know something about your country, something else happens that changes my mind."

"I know of what you speak," said Wonjoon nodding in agreement. "For the past year, I have felt what you have begun to sense. While asleep at night, I have had visions of mysterious changes happening throughout the kingdom. Before I did not think of them much but now I know they have meaning."

There was a lull in the conversation as both parties took in the new information. Finally, Wonjoon continued "We were on a journey to the shrine of *Shén Dào*, with has a special bell inside. We wanted to free the bell from its prison-like state, trapped by petrified vines, which left it incapable of ringing. We thought that by ringing it, somehow these changes in our land would stop.

After we made it to the shrine, we managed to free only some vines and then we were mysteriously transported away. Then, we met a Taoist monk who told us of another land next to ours which is causing the upheaval in our kingdom. He said that the people of this other land are suffering. Their pain is so intense; it is spilling into our kingdom and will soon consume us irrevocably. He told us we need to join two parts of a magical amulet which will keep the peace and harmony in *Hana*."

Wonjoon took out the amulet portion they had received from the monk. He showed it to Simon. A look of recognition came to the blond boy's face. Wonjoon asked "Have you seen something like this before?"

"Yes I think I have seen it," replied Simon. "I was transported, mysteriously, to some other land and came across a piece of metal jewel which could easily fit inside this one. I have to tell you my tale." He then proceeded to tell him of his entire adventure in Hana and the girl he met.

Wonjoon asked "Can you describe this girl?"

Simon responded "Her name is Jaeyin. She was around our age, maybe younger, very thin with dark hair held by a pin. She did not look well-fed at all."

Wonjoon responded "I wonder if that is the same girl I saw in my vision I had before the camping trip." Then Wonjoon told them the details of his vision when he saw Jaeyin.

Their conversation turned to their adventures since they began the camping trip. Wonjoon spoke of the monk they met and what he said about the two separate amulet pieces. At the end Wonjoon said "We are on a quest to find the other amulet half and join them together."

Simon said "It seems that Jaeyin is meant to play an important role and that somehow we need to locate her again so we can join these amulet halves. Can you tell me more of what you know of her?"

Wonjoon said "Yes, in my vision, she seemed to suffer in some place that does not have warmth, unlike our land, *Hana*, which has four seasons. This constant cold weighs heavily upon her heart."

Keeyun, who had been silent up to now, spoke up "Why have you never told me about these dreams Wonja?"

"I did not remember them until know. Only the mention of her by Simon has revived my memory out."

"Oh," responded Keeyun. He remained speechless at the new information and needed some time to digest it.

That evening, the three young boys talked some more and decided they would search for the girl together. They said good night to their hosts and fell fast asleep; each one revisiting in their dreams the thoughts and images they had during the last few days.

CHAPTER SEVENTEEN

Wonjoon woke just before dawn. He went outside and walked up a small hill behind the cabin. He watched the run rise in a clear sky; an event he had seen many times before.

"The sun seems to have lost some of its strength," he noted. He could not feel its heat on his face. Even as it rose higher in the sky, the warmth of the sun's glow eluded Wonjoon.

Worriedly he headed back down to the farmhouse. He stopped in front of a small prayer area. The area had a statue covered by a roof, supported by four beams. He knelt down to say a prayer in silence; a petition to restore things to some form of normalcy. Wonjoon then stood up, bowed, and walked to the farmhouse.

When he came back inside, Simon and Keeyun were up and drinking some green tea. Chuna was preparing some rice and fish for the boys' breakfast. She knew they would need strength for what lay ahead of them.

Having completed his early morning chores, Bae returned to the house and the five of them sat eating the simple meal.

Wonjoon looked outside the window and saw dark clouds coming from the north blocking out the sun. A chill went through his body. The other two boys also noticed the change in temperature.

Chuna prepared some rice rolls for their departure and put it in a small satchel which Keeyun carried.

"Thanks for all you have done for us," said Wonjoon.

"Yes, you have so good to us," responded Simon.

The boys agreed earlier to travel together until they unraveled the secret of the amulet. They also promised to help Simon find his friends.

They walked quietly thinking of things they would encounter as they tried to complete their task. First, they decided to return to Mount Woyeungsan. From there, they would ascend to the temple and look for a way to the other land which Simon had visited.

On the way the elevation started to rise with frost strangely settling on the ground. The weather chilled them as they marched along; feeling improperly dressed for the coldness. While talking their upcoming journey, they realized that a new moon was coming in two days making travel at night nearly impossible.

On the way they saw some interesting things such as a solitary hawk chasing down its prey on a mountainside. Later, a herd of deer rushed past them as they stopped to drink from a mountain stream. They passed small houses in the countryside billowing out smoke as if it was winter.

As they walked through a small village, they saw a parade of women dressed in traditional costumes of purple and white. These women carried on their shoulders pots used for storing food. The boys followed briefly behind them. When they entered the village square, Wonjoon asked the women for some clothing to stay warm. The boys received some leggings, ponchos, and scarves.

They took the clothes to the edge of the village. As they put on them on cold strong winds whipped at their faces. These same winds were making their way to the slopes of Mount Woyeungsan not very far from the village. Looking at the mountain, they saw it was covered with snow, a sharp contrast from Wonjoon's and Keeyun's last visit to it.

Walking was difficult as they ascended on an ice-covered trail. Everything they touched, the leaves and the grass, crunched under their footsteps. They stopped for a brief respite to make hot tea. The brew gave them the needed strength for the final part of their ascent.

They pushed on toward summit. Just before nightfall they arrived at the shrine with enough light allowing the boys to explore it thoroughly. Simon went to the back side of the shrine where he discovered a lower entrance; at a different level than the bell.

Keeyun said "I saw some strong poles planted in the ground just below the crest over there," as he pointed to a lower area. "We can use them to pry or force open the door."

"Okay, Wonja, let's gather them together. I don't know how heavy they'll be," responded Keeyun "So let's work together."

Very short on daylight, they ran down together and gathered up the poles. It was slippery and difficult to maneuver the poles together. They were breathing heavily by the time they finished the lifting and carrying.

"Now let's tie them up at both ends with some of those old vines creeping up the shrine's wall," said Wonjoon.

Keeyun took his small camping knife out of its sheath and began cutting down several vines. The three of them worked until four poles were securely tied together. They decided that using the poles as one solid battering ram was the best way to open the door.

Wonjoon cleared the snow, brush, and rocks from the front of the door. With all the obstructions removed, they had clear access to maneuver the battering ram.

"Okay, let's get to it," he shouted.

The three boys held on to the vines wrapped around the poles as they rushed at the door. They struck it hard making door groan on its hinges.

"Let's just swing it from this position and not run with it anymore. It'll be easier for us to handle in this manner. Hold tight on to the vines," said Wonjoon as he braced himself.

With one boy facing the other two, they swung the tied poles in unison. The poles came crashing down upon the door but it barely moved under the impact.

Keeyun saw a metal bolt fitted into the doorframe which protruded a few centimeters. When they hit the door the second time, Keeyun noticed that the bolt moved slightly to the side.

"Wait one moment," Keeyun said to Wonjoon before they struck it again. "Let's put the poles down for a minute. I want to see something." After they placed the poles on the ground Keeyun picked up a good sized stone which lay a few footsteps away. It was weighty and awkward and he needed two hands to lift it.

"Wonja, move to the side. I don't want to hit you," Keeyun said.

"What are you going to do with that?" Simon asked as he stood behind Keeyun.

"You'll see," Keeyun replied.

He threw it from his shoulder to the bolt on the doorframe. The rock grazed the top of the bolt making it move downward causing the door to shake a little.

"Do it one more time," Wonjoon said supportively.

"Okay, one more hit and it should come loose. Looks very rusty from what I see," said Simon.

Keeyun's next throw landed squarely in the middle of the bolt. A part of the door frame broke around it. The bolt slipped inward a little leaving only its head visible. There it stopped as it became stuck in the wood.

"Okay, now let's strike the door again with the ram. It should be easier now to open," declared Keeyun excitedly.

The boys once again lifted their makeshift battering ram and swinging it a few times and managed to open it leaving a small gap in the doorway. Wonjoon reached inside and unfastened the bulky chain from the eye of the bolt. Relieved of its chain, the door opened freely.

Inside they saw a tunnel leading to an inner chamber not very far away. Reflected sunlight illuminated the chamber. The light made it easier for the boys to walk down the tunnel without hurting themselves on brick protrusions located on the ceiling. They had to crouch down every few steps to avoid low hanging ones.

At the end of the tunnel they saw a room with polished bronze metal covering the walls and ceiling. The illumination came from the openings that stretched all the way to the surface allowing the sunlight to enter. Icicles hung from a few of the skylights and water dripped down off of them making the room cold and damp.

Fourteen hollow copper metal tubes were hung equally apart on the wall of the circular chamber. In the middle of the room two circles of equal size were elevated, a few centimeters higher than the floor, away the wall. These circles bisected each other creating an oval shape between them.

These circles had holes the same size as the tubes. At the intersecting points existed two of these holes. All the holes were separated in an equidistant fashion except for the two extra ones in the inner oval. This inner oval had four tubes separated equally apart in relation to its smaller size.

Seeing many cobwebs hanging, in the room the boys instinctively cut them down using the poles from the wall. They cleared away an area above the circles so they could work.

Wonjoon knelt down to touch one of the mounting spaces and felt its smooth rounded edge. For a few seconds he pondered the design of the place and their next course of action.

After careful thought he said "Let's place the tubes in the holes. I have a feeling this will be our key to freeing up the *Shén Dào*. We just have to figure out how to do it."

"Placing them is the obvious part. How we are going to make them produce a sound is the hard part," said Simon as he placed some of the tubes.

Moments later they had all the tubes securely in place. The three boys walked around them and hit them with their hands. They created a small sound but nothing that lasted.

"What are we not do correctly?" asked Wonjoon. Keeyun went around and inspected the room. "I see nothing else in this room. These tubes are the making of some ancient riddle. They want to be rung but without uncovering their secret we will never be able to do it," he said.

"Let's push on the tubes. Maybe somehow they'll make a sound," speculated Wonjoon.

The boys proceeded to push on some of the tubes without success. Then Keeyun took one of the tubes out of inner oval shape circle. There inside the hole was a metal plate. He put the tube back in to place and looked at the tube across from this one. It too had a metal plate positioned below.

Thinking out loud Keeyun said "I think we are meant to push down on these two tubes."

"Alright, that might be what's needed," responded Wonjoon.

The two boys pushed down on both tubes, simultaneously. They heard a click and a device became activated. A bronze sheet fell across the door entryway. The inner oval slab shape became raised up almost to Keeyun's knee.

Under the slab, two hardened oak staffs revealed themselves. The boys pulled them from their keep.

"This will accomplish what we need, my friends," said Wonjoon. "Kee you go around the outer edge of the poles and started hitting them. Simon and I will stay on the inside of the circles while I use mine."

Wonjoon stepped into the middle and watched as Keeyun started swatting at the poles as he walked. Soon he quickened his pace and vibrations starting, each one leading to stronger louder ones. The sound reached a pitch that became unbearable. Keeyun had to stop and plug his ears with fabric from his sleeve. Wonjoon and Simon covered their ears with their hands.

When Keeyun started again hitting the tubes the room began to shake from the sound vibrations. Even the ground began to tremble under these conditions. Keeyun stopped when he realized that the vibrations were growing without his help.

As the chamber continued to shake, the boys fell to the floor. Wonjoon yelled at his two friends "Let's get out of here. It isn't safe." Keeyun saw Wonjoon talking but could not make out his words.

The sound bothered Keeyun so much he quickly lifted up the bronze sheet and slid to the other side of the entryway. The sound continued reverberating making his ears bleed. He kept his hands pressed against them until a bright light flashed making him fall. The whole place turned eerily silent.

Keeyun lay there a minute to gather his wits. Finally he stood up and went back into the chamber, pushing the bronze plate out of the way. The room had changed because the sun had descended away from the skylights; leaving it much darker.

Keeyun could not see well and called out "Wonjoon, Simon, where are you?" His friends did not answer. Worriedly he went through the entire chamber searching, only to find it empty except for the tubes and the two wooden staffs on the floor.

Keeyun went back outside and thought for a few moments. Not knowing now what to do, he walked up to the Shrine's entrance. The sunlight was getting close to the horizon shining directly at the bell. Keeyun thought that maybe he could now free the bell. He went up to the top of the shrine and started to pull at every vine he could reach. They were brittle and became dust in his hands. In a matter of several minutes the vines were down and the bell was free.

The sky darkened and Keeyun decided to wait until morning to clean the shrine more thoroughly. Then, after not seeing any signs of his friends he decided to descend and find his way home.

CHAPTER EIGHTEEN

Wonjoon found himself on a trail illuminated by a faint yellowish indescribable glow. It reflected off the white surface of the footpath giving the trail an eerie look.

Wonjoon saw the path was wide and went downward in what appeared to be large spirals. After taking a few steps, he slipped and lost his footing. The path had frost on it which Wonjoon had not seen because the yellow glow masked over it. He felt the crystal coldness on the ground as he came to an abrupt and harsh stop, bruising his left hand in the process.

As Wonjoon looked around, he saw Simon hurling down upon him. Out of control, he knocked Wonjoon further down the path. They slid together for a few seconds before coming to a complete rest.

Using his bruised left hand as a brake Wonjoon began to bleed and blister. They both stopped at the edge of the pathway. Wonjoon looked down over the edge and saw that they were on a spiral pathway which continued to narrow below them.

Wonjoon turned to Simon and asked "Is this the way you went on your previous trip?"

"I told you how I escaped. The way collapsed behind me so it can't be this. Also, this way is much colder. The other time, the temperature was very mild," responded Simon.

At the same moment the boys sat there on the cold trail, the Pon Guards led Jaeyin into the caverns of Musihan. For the past several decades, these caverns had become infamous in *Bun Dan* as the place of final punishment which was meted out to malcontents, dissenters, and criminals alike.

The caverns connect to the Fortress City by way of an underground tunnel. Several centuries earlier, a mining party discovered these caverns under the rocky and imposing Mount Kwun Yung. The Ruler decided to dig the connecting tunnel for two reasons; first, to provide an escape for himself and his closest advisors if needed and secondly, for viewing the punishment of those convicted.

Engineers for the Ruler devised a terraced viewing area above the Chamber of Reckoning where they dispensed the punishment. The important spectators who assembled on the terrace could view the events from a comfortable and safe vantage point.

Lit torches and specially designed mirrors were placed in the adjoining tunnels and side chambers. Their placement was part of an ingenious system whereby images of the activities beyond the main chamber became visible. They reflected images into the great chamber onto other mirrors that were hung there. The onlookers on the terrace had clear views of the events happening at various places simultaneously.

As the evening began, dignitaries and generals arrived, mingled, and feasted. They ate roasted mutton, drank fine blueberry wine as they waited for the event to start. Two musicians, a man and a woman dressed in purple colored robes with white fringes, came in to play traditional music. Each strummed an identical three stringed instrument.

A trumpet sounded and the lower gate opened. Barefoot prisoners walked in single file through the entrance bound to each other by shackles. Within the group, Jaeyin walked third back from the lead prisoner.

The lead guard had them stand and face the crowd on the terrace. As the onlookers gazed at the prisoners, three guards began releasing them from their shackles.

A High Court Crier stood at the edge of the terrace and announced the crimes of each prisoner. The court scheduled other criers to make the same announcement in the main square of the Fortress City and neighboring villages at the same time. These types of announcements helped the government control the people and limit further dissention.

The Crier added these words after stating their crimes "This is a special day which has deep meaning to each inhabitant of *Bun Dan*. This day we celebrate our founding in history and the stability our land has achieved. Once, a long time ago, our land was besieged by invaders from abroad. Only through the wisdom and mercy of the Great Pon have we been able to overcome those invaders to live now in peace."

He turned to address those convicted below "You, who have defiled our land with your foul acts and seditious words with the intention of subverting the very peace and stability we enjoy, will have your sentences carried out. But, because today is a special day, you will have a chance to live. You may win your lives back and receive exile if you successfully go through these tunnels and find a way out. Only through the benevolence of our great ruler, Pon Cho Hun, is such a gift awarded. Remember that if you manage to escape, you cannot return to *Bun Dan*. If you do, it will mean your instant death."

The lead guard uttered the word "Go." At first the prisoners did not understand. The first prisoner cautiously moved past the lead guard and looked around. As he got closer to one of the two tunnels on the far side, he ran. The rest of the prisoners understood that they were meant to do and also ran. When the entire group of prisoners had left the chamber, the guards collected the chains from the floor and exited through a thick metal reinforced door under the terrace.

Most of the prisoners followed into the very same tunnel. However, Jaeyin entered the opposite one. A few seconds later, one prisoner, an older bespectacled man, decided to follow her instead of the large group.

Jaeyin removed a torch hanging on the wall and began to run swiftly. She knew that to be as far away from the main chamber, when they released the beasts, was her best chance at survival.

Back in the main chamber, two guards opened a gated entrance to a small cave. One guard, carrying a torch, went in and turned a wheel that opened another gate further inside. He threw the torch on the ground and ran out of the cave following his partner to the exit which the other guards had used. When they reached it someone opened the door and let them enter. Safely inside, they quickly closed and bolted the door in two places.

Growls started to come from the small cave. Beasts moved towards the torch slowly, feeling their way, determining if any threat existed.

Three grisly trutorjin emerged from the cave. The crowd above remained silent and motionless. Two of the dog-beasts heard the sound of moving feet down the tunnel where most of the prisoners had chosen to go. The dog beasts walked up to the tunnels snarling and growling as they sniffed the scent of the prisoners. They sensed more than just the prisoners' odor in the air; they sensed their fear which unleashed their ferocity. The desire for flesh overwhelmed two of the beasts making them leap into the tunnel with a roar as they began the pursuit.

The solitary trutorjin became interested in the other tunnel. Jaeyin stopped running when she heard the growls of the two dog beasts enter the other cave. The man following behind her stopped to listen also. He too, was carrying another torch that hung at the entrance. She put her finger to her lips to signal him to be quiet. Together they waited, trying to hear what was happening in the main chamber.

They heard the growls of the two beasts that went into the other tunnel becoming fainter until only silence remained.

Jaeyin thought it was safe to go. As she turned to leave, the man stumbled over a rock. That rock hit another larger one making a sound that traveled down the tunnel.

The beast heard the faint sound in the distance and gave out a chilling growl. It raced into the tunnel to find the maker of the noise.

After realizing the animal had begun to pursue them, Jaeyin started to run. She turned her head to the side as she ran, shouting to the man "Run quickly sir, that beast will be upon us shortly."

Her feet took her quickly through the tunnel. The man wearing glasses ran as fast as he could behind her. Sweat fogged up his lenses and made his running difficult. He breathed heavily because he was not used to strenuous exercise.

Jaeyin reached a point where the tunnel forked into two separate ones. She slowed down for a second and then decided to follow the one to her left. The old man was thirty steps behind her. As she made the turn, he was able to follow only by the trail of light coming from her torch.

Jaeyin noticed the ceiling getting lower and the width of the tunnel getting narrower. After more than a minute of running, she had to crouch forward to move through the tunnel, slowing down her pace.

Up ahead the tunnel became even narrower, making it necessary for her to crawl through it. She felt glad that the way was constricted because she thought that it would prevent the beast from following. Dropping his torch out of fear made the old man completely dependent on Jaeyin's movements. He quickly caught up to her and followed alongside.

Simon and Wonjoon went slowly down the spiral pathway for a short while; slipping and falling many times due to the ice. Further below, the air temperature became warmer. With the ice and frost finally gone, they were able to run.

The spiral pathway entered into a cave. At the entrance the boys stopped to rest and think.

"Here, let's use these matches I have," said Simon "And make torches from our clothes."

Simon ripped off the bottoms of both sides of his trousers and lit them. Handing one miniature torch to Wonjoon he said "These won't last long. So we must go quickly. Remember to stay close to me."

"Yes, Simon," responded Wonjoon. As he took the amulet half out of his pocket, he felt it start to vibrate. A slight glow emanated from the amulet. He held it up to show Simon and said "This must mean we're getting close to where we need to be."

Simon responded "I know the amulet needs to be here. But I am not too sure about us."

Upon those last words, the boys entered the tunnel with their makeshift torches. The entrance had hundreds of cobwebs lining it. The boys burnt them away as they lifted their torches in the front of their bodies.

No sooner had they begun walking than they came upon a small boulder blocking their path.

"This can't be the way," said Wonjoon in a frustrated voice.

"Don't worry. I think we can move this boulder. It looks like it was deliberately placed here to block the way," said Simon responding to Wonjoon's objection.

"You may be right," answered Wonjoon. "Okay, let's try it."

They pushed at the boulder from the right side until it budged a little, leaving a small opening big enough for them to crawl through. Wonjoon bent down and extended his arm with the amulet into the space. He saw a few rats scurry away into the dusty stale air inside.

"Okay, the way is ready. Are you going first?" asked Simon.

"Yes, I will take the lead from now on," Wonjoon answered as he crawled inside with Simon following close behind.

As they crouched down because of the low ceiling, their torches extinguished themselves. In the darkness Wonjoon felt the amulet vibrating in his hand. The light it gave off became stronger the farther they went into the tunnel. Soon it was strong enough to see several meters ahead.

After crawling on hands and knees for fifteen minutes, they saw a bright light ahead of them which led them to the well-lit chamber. Once inside the chamber they were relieved to be out in the open space because the tunnel restrictive size had caused their backs to ache.

This large place of which they entered was called the Tajii Chamber; a place constructed long ago and hidden well beneath Mount Kwun Yung. The boys sensed that this place may be their destination of their quest.

With the torch burning out, Jaeyin and the man were forced to stop. As their eyes adjusted to the darkness, Jaeyin felt a strange pulsing sensation touching her abdomen. She pulled out the chain that held the amulet from inside her clothes and for some reason it was pulsating and giving off a faint glow.

As she looked around with the light from the amulet, she saw how the dust filled the air causing her a reflex reaction of making her cough. As they moved around more tiny particles filled the space they occupied. The dryness of the air almost choked her. She covered her mouth and tried to stay motionless. The man did the same.

They heard a growl come from behind them. The sound of her cough must have reached the ears of the beast. Her heart leaped when it roared seconds later. The roar echoed off the walls up ahead of them.

The man grabbed her shoulder from behind and said "There's no time. We need to move fast!"

"I agree. Let's move as fast as possible. I think the large beast is moving slower because of his size but it will still be able to reach us," responded Jaeyin.

Jaeyin moved further down the tunnel. Before the man started to follow her, he picked up the extinguished torch.

The two of them moved quickly in their crouched positions; several times hitting their heads on the tunnel ceiling above.

They stopped a minute later to listen for the animal. Jaeyin noticed that the amulet had become more illuminated. As she examined the piece of metal, horrid growls came from behind them; from one of the turns they had just passed.

Before they had a chance to move, the beast came at them with incredible force. The man turned to face the beast putting his body between it and Jaeyin. He swung the unlit torch at the animal and hit it squarely on the head sending the beast against the wall.

He yelled at her to go as fast as she could. She followed his instruction and went quickly through the cramped tunnel.

The man must be putting up a good fight, she thought, as she managed to further herself in the tunnel. But suddenly, she heard cries of agony and knew that the beast had killed him and would now come for her.

As this thought passed through her mind, Jaeyin came to a junction with three separate tunnels. The tunnel to her right had a faint distant light while the other two were completely dark. She decided that the light would give her the best chance of escape.

Jaeyin let the amulet swing freely from her neck as she ran. The tunnel became larger. Once more the growl of the beast filled her ears. Fear consumed her, making her run faster.

She followed the light into a large chamber. As she entered, she looked to her right and saw a strange sight. In the middle of the great room moved a horrific looking tusked elephant. The large animal appeared blinded as mucous seeped from its eyes. It wore a harness with blackened spikes around its underside and head. She could see the animal moved with agony and pain. Compassion immediately stirred in her heart for the animal.

Jaeyin took a few steps into the chamber and noticed a metal gate that swung open from the tunnel she had just exited. She grabbed the gate and swung it until it was closed. She slid a bolt, which was halfway from the floor, into a thick metal casing.

"I hope that holds," she said out loud. She backed away from the gate as the beast finally reached her. It slammed headfirst into the metal bar of the gate. The mighty beast became incensed and hit the gate several more times. The gate was strong and held fast.

Jaeyin followed the wall away from the tunnel; keeping one hand on the wall's surface as she looked into the great chamber. She saw the master, the driver of the elephant. He was a hideous bearded dwarf who swung a whip in the air, snapping it behind the elephant's head. He paced back and forth in a space above the animal while muttering obscenities.

The dwarf had dirty brown hair that hung down to his belly. He had grime and dirt all over his clothes and body and wore a black metal helmet. The helmet's visor was pushed to the back of his neck. Much of his filthy hair protruded from the helmet giving him a ghoulish look Also, the skin on his hands and face were the color of blackened ash which showed how intently he did his work for the Great Pon; never once stopping for a rest.

The dwarf forced the elephant, by whip, through a rut that separated the sacred Tajii circle from the rest of the room.

An ancient people had created this circle as a peace talisman two millennia ago. They foresaw the dangers of the changing world and wanted to leave a blessing behind. They built the Tajii to keep the bonds of the natural order of life upon the Earth intact. This tribute, a gift to the future, was the last thing they did before mysteriously disappearing. They left no other trace of their existence on the entire planet.

Pon Cho Hut learned of this place from the Conjurer. He realized that to create the vision of the world he wanted he needed to destroy this talisman. He located the Tajii a few years after the kingdom divided. He set into motion, through the use of dark magic, to bring about its destruction no matter how long it took.

He used the dwarf who has worked without interruption up until the present time. Many beasts and enchantments have been used over the last century to destroy the Tajii. Today that wish was about to become reality as the task was almost finished.

The dwarf had gone mad long ago. Still he labored under his original directive in a relentless manner.

The elephant moved back and forth with a grinding machine attached to its large head; cutting into the stone under the sacred circle. One of the two bridges that stretched from the main floor to the circle was about to give way. When this happens, said the legend, the blessing which the circle bestowed upon the planet would slip away leaving mankind defenseless.

The elephant was pulled back by the dwarf for the final strike at the stone bridge spanning to the sacred circle. Jaeyin carefully crossed the bridge so it would not give way under her feet.

At the sacred circle, Jaeyin saw Wonjoon enter the great chamber from the other side of the circle. Simon also entered and looked out on the events happening without going any further. They both looked up and saw Jaeyin in a precarious position. Wonjoon called out "Jaeyin."

The sound of her name alerted the dwarf to her presence. The dwarf expressed his displeasure at her by making an awful sound which made Jaeyin fall backward.

She grasped at the wall to stop herself from going into the rut close to the elephant.

Wonjoon, seeing her fall, ran swiftly across the bridge and grabbed her by both hands and lifted her upward.

The whip sounded again and the elephant moved toward the bridge Jaeyin had crossed. On impact, it started to shake and crumble. The bridge on the other side of the sacred circle gave way also. Then, the whole earth began to tremble as both bridges lay in waste.

As rocks fell from the ceiling, Wonjoon knew they had little time left. He saw the Jaeyin's amulet half hanging from the chain around her neck. He said to her "Quickly, we must go to the center and place our amulet pieces together."

The two of them moved swiftly to the center as the stone circle became quite unsteady. Jaeyin took off the chain from around her neck and handed it to Wonjoon. He put both pieces together as the shaking of the great room made him fall to the side of the small pedestal in the center. He pushed himself up and placed the amulet in a cut out groove at the center of the pedestal. It fit perfectly.

Together, and in place, the amulet started to emanate a great light. The pedestal began to grow higher as the rocks from the ceiling fell around it; growing so tall it cut through the hard rock above. The pedestal continued upward to the slopes of the mountain. As it came to the surface, it sent out a great white light that went through the darkened sky. It burnt away the clouds with one bright explosive burst.

At the explosion, Simon tumbled back into the tunnel he had just left, which protected him from the falling rocks and dirt. Several large rocks fell in the entryway blocking out the light from the chamber. He decided that he needed to get back into the chamber to find his friends. He dug steadily in the darkness for a while before breaking through.

Crawling into the faintly lit chamber, he saw the pedestal had returned to its original position. The sacred circle no longer had a carved rut around it. Instead the ground was even and smooth.

Wonjoon and Jaeyin were nowhere to be seen. Yet the amulet still remained positioned on the pedestal which provided light to the entire chamber. Simon looked around for clues as to the whereabouts of his friends. None were visible.

He opened the gate which Jaeyin had locked. There, the trutorjin lay crushed under a boulder. Simon retraced the way Jaeyin had entered only to find the great Fortress City in ruin and abandoned. From there he went south in search of the crew of sailors he had left behind.

CHAPTER NINETEEN

Simon walked through the main gate that led into the Fortress City and saw residents with their belongings outside. He walked up to one group and saw a thin older man trying to convince a small group of people to some course of action.

"Excuse me, Sir," Simon said as he tapped his shoulder.

Startled, the man turned around and stared at Simon for a second. He blinked his eyes adjusted to this strange sight; a common reaction from most people in this part of the world due to the color of his hair. He had grown accustomed to it.

"What are you doing here?" asked the man.

"Sir, I have come here with my friend through the caverns that lay below your city. Some misfortune has occurred to him and a girl we met."

"Who is this girl you speak of?" said the man with sudden interest.

Simon replied "She is called Jaeyin. I met her briefly a while back and gave her an amulet half I had found in some pool. My friend, who by chance carried the other half of the amulet, and she joined the amulet halves together in the Tajii Chamber. Then I lost sight of them as the rocks from the ceiling began to fall."

The man put both hand on his heart as he heard the last words of the boy. "That girl you describe is my daughter. She went into the Pit of Treachery today, those are the caverns of which you speak," said the man. "I would like to introduce myself. My name is Yoona."

As he talked he waved at a woman to come over to them. "This here is my wife Hee-Un." Turning to his spouse he told her "Dear, this boy has seen our daughter. She escaped those beasts and found herself deep in the mountain."

"Yes," said Simon as he bowed to Jaeyin's mother. "But she along and my friend have disappeared. I am sorry I wasn't able to do more. When they joined together the two separate pieces of the amulet they carried they placed it on some pedestal. It burst through the ceiling. After that I lost sight of them as the rocks fell and blocked my vision. I looked for them in the chamber afterwards and couldn't find any signs of them. I wish I knew if they were alright or not."

"Thank you my boy," replied Hee-Un. "Your story gives me comfort that at least Jaeyin did not suffer at the touch of those beasts. My heart has felt terrible pain because I was not allowed to see her. Also thinking of her anguish was unbearable. We were so powerless to help to her!" With those last words tears ran down her cheek as the recent memory entered her thoughts. She had to step away from her husband and Simon.

Yoona went over and grabbed her shoulders for support. As they whispered some dark clouds formed in the northern half of the sky. The southern half still remained filled with the bright summer sun. The clouds seemed to rise up out the city itself. They grew in size and soon covered the peak of Mount Kwun Yung from the area behind the Fortress City. They passed upward and over the top of the mountain, cutting through and dissipating the clouds. The people around them talking became silent as they each turned to stare at the colored arch. Never had one appeared in their land due to the sky always carrying some shade. But today with the bright bluish hue above them they saw the world anew.

"Come with me," said Simon. I want to show you the land to the south. It will surprise you as you see its richness. A big difference from the barrenness I see here."

"Okay, let's go," said Yoona.

Jaeyin's father turned and addressed the people in their language. He told them of their intentions and asked if any would like to join in.

Many families that did not have missing members followed them as they made their trek south. Some decided to stay and look for loved ones or return to their homes.

The newly formed group of about a hundred people made their way south. Yoona explained that the Fortress City was near the northern border of the kingdom and that their journey would take a few days to reach the southern portion. He recommended that they take shelter in a soldier's garrison for the evening.

The garrison was the site of a monastery converted to house soldiers when the old ways in *Bun Dan* were outlawed. The Pon Brethren replaced any monks in the land. It became a crime to mention the old religions that the people once followed. So many monks were put to their death during the great purge at the founding of *Bun Dan*.

As they entered the garrison which still carried the feeling of its ancient predecessors they found no trace of soldiers or their weapons. As it was at the Fortress City no remnants of the military or government officials existed.

The group found abundant food in the garrison's kitchen. The ruler was notoriously for keeping his soldiers well fed even when famine was upon the land. Cho Hun knew that his power resided in his military and carefully nurtured them to maintain his grip.

They roasted some meat found hanging in the food locker and prepared a feast of rice and vegetables. Some in the group scrounged around looking for things of value while others prepared their sleeping area.

They built a big fire in the general area where the soldiers used to spend their evenings. As they ate they felt the nutrients in the food work their effect on their bodies. Many had not eaten well in their lives which had affected their stature and muscles. Yoona was taller than the rest due to his earlier life of prestige.

As the food lifted their spirits they talked about how they would change the land. First, by electing leaders and making councils that would oversee the task needed in building up their country. They started to believe that they could work together and create something much different than they had known. The food they found gave them this new found energy and hope.

During the night they all slept soundly under a waning moonlight coming through the windows of the soldier's dormitories.

In the morning, several families decided to stay in the area and visit the local village. They felt that they should begin building new houses here as the land appeared more fertile. They would use the garrison as temporary lodging until their construction had ended. Also, they would encourage other wanderers that it was time to begin life anew and settle in the area.

Simon, Yoona, and Hee-Un set out with only two families comprised of no more than ten people. They all felt compelled to continue south to this other land because of the descriptions Simon told. They had suffered tremendously under Cho Hun, losing several family members due to disease or arrest by the Pon Brethren. They wanted to distant themselves from the place of their bad memories and see a brighter world.

CHAPTER TWENTY

The King of the south saw the great light shine in the sky. When it had finished the cloud that obstructed his and his subject's vision cleared. Stunned, they saw what had eluded their eyes for so long that the Pon with the help of the Conjurer's dark powers had managed to convince the people of the north and south realms that they had no neighbors. Now the way between them became clear and people started filtering into both sides. The King set out to look at this new land with seven guards and his most favored friend Lord Ata.

He rode from the capital city to the Mount Woyeungsan deciding to make the pilgrimage to its' famous shrine before venturing any further north. As the group came up to the Haneen River they came upon a boy trudging tiredly on the trail. The king sensed something important about this boy and ordered his men to halt.

The boy collapsed in exhaustion front of the King's stallion. Dismounting quickly, the King went to the Boy. His personal guard did likewise coming immediately to the side of his highness, as was his duty.

Taking out his water canteen, the King kneeled over the boy and ran water over the boy's mouth. Some water entered the boy's wind pipe which made him lean up and begin to cough. When his episode subsided he reached for the canteen to take a swig of the water.

The guard became alert when the boy reached out to the King and unsheathed a small sword he carried. The King said "Put that away, he is too tired to do your King much harm. This boy is only in need of water and some rest."

"Boy, can you hear me?" he asked.

"Yes, your grace," he replied.

"Can you tell me your name and how is it that you came here and in such terrible condition?"

"Yes, I was trying to find my camping friends when I became disoriented. I came across the ferry near here and crossed our great river. As I left the ferry I heard a noise from behind. Turning to sound I saw a great light that nearly blinded me I fell down and crawled to the nearby tree. I sat there for more than a day until my eye sight returned. Then I set out no more than a few hours ago to find my way home. That is when you came upon me."

"What is your name boy and where is your home?" asked his highness.

"My name is Keeyun and I am from your humble village Pujon," replied the boy.

The king motioned to the guard to move the boy off the trail and onto the grass.

The King said "Everyone dismount, we will wait until this boy is feeling fine. Let us rest until tomorrow."

They set up camp on the roadside; one tent for the King and one for the boy. They let the boy sleep in the King's tent until dinner was prepared. When they all sat around the fire Keeyun felt strong enough to tell his highness of his adventures.

The King listened intently and decided that tomorrow they would make their way to the Shrine before venturing any further. He had visited the Shrine a few times when younger but had lost interest in it as his duties as ruler became difficult and time consuming.

The king commanded the boy to lead them the way back he had come. Keeyun rode doubled up on a horse with one of the guards back to the ferry. Arriving, the royal party discovered an unmanned ferry. The king feeling impatient ordered his guards aboard and commandeered the ferry across the river.

Once on the northern side, the group followed the path that led to the Keeyun's original campsite with his fellow villagers. The King ordered his guards and lord to stay behind and set up camp and asked his personal guard to accompany up the slopes of Mount Woyeungsan. The three took to the trail the King was too impatient to wait another day.

The King and his personal guard rode resolutely up the mountain even though the shale slopes made it difficult for their horses to keep their footing. Halfway up, they jumped off their horses and pulled on their reins to lead the prized animals upward.

Darkness began to settle over the land and guard lit a torch to guide them up the last of the way.

When they reached firmer ground they remounted and walked their horses slowly. Keeyun was surprised by how shrine radiate in the waning moonlight. Its silhouette made it seem even grander.

Keeyun showed the way underneath the central part of the shrine where he had lost his two friends. The guard entered first to make sure everything was secure. He called back "Your grace, come quickly. I think I have found someone."

The King and Keeyun raced down the tunnel to see the guard standing over two bodies.

"Your grace, it turns out that there are two people. They appear to be of the same age as Keeyun."

Keeyun ran over and discovered one was Wonjoon. His hands were holding on to that of a girl and facing her. Excitedly, Keeyun talked to his friend "Wake up, wake up."

The king joined them and said "We need to take them outside." The guard lifted the girl and Keeyun carried his friend.

Outside, under the moonlight glow they saw that the two youngsters were still alive. The king said "We had best carry them slowly down the mountain. I am sorry we have no more time to examine the shrine but we need care for these young ones at a lower elevation."

"Yes, your grace. I place the boy on my lap as I ride."

"Good, I will tie my steed to the back of yours and carry the girl. Keeyun, you lead the horses down. Let us not delay," the King commanded.

They spent the rest of the night descending slowly. Jaeyin came back to semi-consciousness in the King's arms. She moaned softly in her weakened condition.

"There, there my child, you are safe. We are almost at our camp. Once we have arrived you will be taken care of and fed; my dear," he said comforting her.

They arrived at camp at the break of dawn. The Lord Ata was relieved to see his grace return; having feared something might have happened to the small riding party.

Keeyun slept at the side of his friend and the girl. The King also went to sleep for few hours to recuperate. They all slept till sun passed the noon sky.

A guard see they were awake invited the three young ones to come to the campfire to eat.

"You go, Keeyun," said Wonjoon. "I will be right with you."

With Keeyun gone, Wonjoon asked "Are you feeling well enough to eat with these strangers. I will be by you side the whole time."

"Yes, I'll be okay, and I am rather hungry," said Jaeyin as she grabbed on Wonjoon's arm.

Keeyun was already eating when the two arrived. They all ate in silence. When Wonjoon felt some strength return, he said "Keeyun, I cannot tell you how glad I am to see you again. I want to introduce you to the girl Simon talked about, who he met and gave the other amulet half to. She and I met up in this grand chamber under a mountain up north. There we saw this incredible elephant beast try to destroy the sacred circle. As the whole place was falling apart we managed to put the two amulet halves together and place them into a pedestal. Then we were consumed by light and the next we knew you were waking us at shrine here."

The girl turned to Keeyun and put one hand on Wonjoon's hand and said "Yes, that is all I remember too.

We have stories in *Bun Dan*, my land, about that chamber and its sacred circle called the Tajii. I thought they were a myth. But they proved to be true."

"Well I am happy to meet you Jaeyin and see you are doing well. Do either of you know what happened to Simon? For a stranger to our land he has done so much."

"Yes, I also would like to know what happened to him," answered the King who approached.

"I don't know. I lost sight of him and haven't seen since."

They talked for the rest of the afternoon until the King saw that his two new guests needed some more rest. The two went to sleep some more as the King and his Lord talk about their next plans.

CHAPTER TWENTY ONE

The next morning, the guards, following the King's orders, broke camp and followed the path up the river's bank into the northern land.

They passed many people along the way. These strangers to the King's realm spoke the same language, but with a different inflection and many word not used in *Hana*. These people passed the royal party not knowing it was his royal highness and therefore spoke freely. They expressed their desire to go south and see the land beyond their border.

The King knew that if the numbers of these people increased in his kingdom that *Hana* would have problem. He felt torn between going south to set up reception areas for these refugees and journeying farther north to learn for himself about this strange neighboring land.

Earlier, Wonjoon had woken complaining of pain in his stomach and neck His discomfort grew as he traveled bravely with the royal entourage. But it became apparent after a few hours that his condition had worsened. Worried, the King called a halt to their ride and decided that his men need set up camp quickly so they could properly care for the boy.

As they made camp his royal highness ordered his Lord Ata to go south to a nearby garrison and return with half its' soldiers. He ordered the soldiers that remained in the garrison to construct a camp to house refugees fleeing south. Additionally, the lord was to instruct the garrison's captain that food and provisions be provided in sufficient amounts to satisfy at least two thousand people over the next month.

The King saw the flow of people passing by and believed the numbers could easily swell to the thousands. These people would need an area to live in. If the lord could start a camp now problems for his kingdom could become avoided; he hoped.

Feeling better because of his decision the king retired for the evening into his tent. He left one guard skilled in medicine to watch over of Wonjoon in the Lord's tent.

Jaeyin also slept in the same tent. After an attempt to stay awake and care for Wonjoon fell she fell asleep at his side. Keeyun and the guard applied water to Wonjoon's forehead continually during their vigil. By midnight the guard convinced Keeyun to sleep as he alone cared for his friend.

An hour later the guard noticed Wonjoon's condition escalating. The boy's forehead had become red from the fever making him say strange things from a state of delirium.

The guard had to move Jaeyin farther away from Wonjoon so he could better care for the boy. Several times he had to soak the boy with a pot of water collected from the riverside.

Wonjoon's mind separated from his body, forced out by his delirium, and was able to enter a vision state similar to the time he had seen Jaeyin for the first time.

In this manner Wonjoon found himself running down a dusty and isolated rocky road that traversed a mountainside. He ran with his head down feeling desperate and completely bewildered. He heard a rock fall from overhead and stopped. A large boulder crossed his path no more than five meters ahead.

He said "That was close. Thanks to heaven I stopped when I did or I would have been down there falling alongside that boulder."

Wonjoon saw a figure in the distance waiting for him. It was Jaeyin who stood there at the entrance to a footbridge that spanned across a stream below. As Wonjoon approached her she lifted her right hand, palm facing him, and touched his forehead. Her hand was cool to the touch and his whole body immediately felt a sense of ease and calm.

Reassuringly, she said to him "You're condition has improved I see; for than I am glad."

Wonjoon said "Yes, whatever I had seems to have passed. I think your touch has done it."

"Maybe," she responded thoughtfully. "Now it is time to go," the girl said and cupped her right hand in that of Wonjoon's left one. As she held tight on to him the land moved under their feet and they passed over the bridge. They floated quickly up over a pass and down into a nearby valley.

The sun, shining briefly, illuminated a large amount of people camping near some castle. Then darkness fell as the boy and girl floated to the entry way of the castle. They passed through the gates without incident and went down a long corridor. Coming to the door a dormitory they settled upon the floor.

Jaeyin peered inside the doorway and was surprised to see Simon resting upon a bed bunk. She recognized him immediately by his hair color. She tugged on Wonjoon and said "Look, it's our friend."

Puzzled, for a moment he was not sure what he was looking at. As he walked closer the moonlight shined on the boy's hair and he too knew it was Simon. The two of them bent over Simon trying to wake him by touching on his chest. Their hands passed right through Simon as if they were phantoms. Frustrated Jaeyin called out "Simon, Simon, it is us, your friends Jaeyin and Wonjoon. Can you hear us?"

Dismayed at their lack of success the two turned away to inspect the rest of the room. Surprise overwhelmed Jaeyin as she recognized her mother and father sleeping together on a bunk bed opposite Simon.

She ran over to her mother and called out "Mami, it is me, your loving daughter. Jaeyin felt joy to know her parent were safe along with their friend.

Feeling content Wonjoon said to Jaeyin "I think it is time we go back. Now that we know they are okay we can start looking for them when we awake."

"Yes, I want to go back and convince the king to escort us here," responded Jaeyin. At the last remark she turned toward the door and took flight along with Wonjoon through the corridor, returning south over the pass until they reached the tent which held their sleeping bodies. As they passed back into their flesh they felt the warm pull of gravity take hold of them.

They arrived at dawn as the sun took followed a path upward in the sky. It was as this time that Wonjoon's fever broke. Feeling better but still groggy he sat up and stretched.

The guard who patiently attended to the boy walked back to the King's tent to tell him the good news.

The boys went down to the river to wash up some and then returned to campfire area. Jaeyin, already seated on a tree stump, was already eating. The boys filled up a bowl each and sat in front of Jaeyin. As they began to chat the King entered the area.

"So, I hope you had a well-deserved rest last night?" asked the King.

"Yes, we did for the most part. But we had a vision. Jaeyin and I together well asleep sort of dreamt the same thing," said Wonjoon.

"Oh, you must tell me over breakfast,' said the King. His attendant prepared a bowl of a simple meal and brought it as the King sat on stump.

"Well your highness, you see we have just been talking about our dreams or visions and found them to be the same," started Jaeyin.

Wonjoon added "We met in front of a stone bridge up on a trail that we are sure was up north. Together we traveled to the valley beyond it and found a multitude of people in a camp."

Jaeyin added "There was some castle nearby in which we entered. To our surprise we found our friend Simon and my parents sleeping in the same room."

"Do you think what you two saw was real or some concoction of the mind?" asked the King.

"We both remember the same details your Highness. We believe that we did indeed travel there. But not in our bodies," said Wonjoon.

"And I am happy that I have seen my parents alive. I know they are well and that we will see each other again," said Jaeyin.

"Good, I am content that from what you have seen. You did not mention seeing any soldiers in the castle or outside it. Were there any?" asked the King.

"No sir, there were no sentries or any sign of soldiers in the area," answered Wonjoon.

CHAPTER TWENTY TWO

After breakfast the King's party broke camp and continued their journey north. The group traveled slowly talking to the people along the route. The King stopped and spoke to them, encouraging them to return to their homes and not abandon their country. He promised *Hana* would send aid once he learned what they needed.

The following day a company of two hundred soldiers arrived under the command of Lord Ata. They carried with them four wagons of supplies; to be used in assisting as many people as they could.

The lord advised the King "More supplies are being gathered, but I do not believe we have enough from the likes of the amount of people we are seeing, your grace."

"Yes, well we must convince them not to readily abandon their homes. I do not find any traces of the soldiers from this Cho Hut they talk about. It is fear of their sudden freedom that weighs heavily on their minds, giving them doubt about their own abilities. We must convince them to return to their homes and start their lives again. I am sure they will see reason soon enough when they learn that we, their brothers to the south, supported them and wanted to live in peaceful trade with them."

Later that day the King and his entourage arrived at a town called Weeshon. The King convinced a few elders to house the Lord Ata as his ambassador.

Having seen enough, the King decided to return to the capital city and discuss with his advisers further details of their assistance. He felt satisfied that the people posed no threat to *Hana*. Also, if they could assistance they would regain their self-sufficiency.

Lord Ata ordered that no one from *Hana* could go beyond Weeshon without his knowledge and consent. Even though Jaeyin was anxious to find her parents she obeyed the Lord.

A few days later, Simon along with Jaeyin's parents arrived at the town. The guards were on the lookout for the blond-haired boy after the lord provided them with a description. When the three arrived, the guards immediately led them to Wonjoon, Keeyun, and Jaeyin. A reunion filled with joy.

Lord Ata met with Jaeyin's father, Yoona, and discovered that he was a very well educated man. Seeing how his abilities may prove beneficial to both lands, the lord selected Yoona as the official liaison between people of *Bun Dan* and *Hana*. The elders in Weeshon agreed to Yoona as the appropriate choice.

Soon after the happy reunion, the three boys asked for permission to return south. Keeyun and Wonjoon told the lord that their families must be worried as to the reason for their prolonged absence. Simon said the same thing about his friends.

Simon asked for special papers to travel to the capital city and get help in locating the crew members from the HSS Emerald.

The Lord prepared the papers and put his personal seal on them. He knew the King would want to have an audience with Simon as soon as possible so sent the three on their way the next day.

It was difficult goodbye for Jaeyin and Wonjoon. But they promised to write and see each other again.

EPILOGUE

As peace spread through the land the people of *Bun Dan* started many local councils. Together they elected some leaders to go to the capital city in *Hana*. In the meantime, life became better over the next several months and winter saw more plentiful food in *Bun Dan* than had ever been seen before by the peasants.

The following year, feeling a special kinship to the people of the south, the residents of Bun asked to become integrated into *Hana*. The people and the King agreed and on the next mid-summer festival they celebrated the joining of the two lands.

The King granted the northerners the right to have self-governing bodies; the only real change was trade and the free movement of people throughout the kingdom.

The King even suggested renaming the kingdom to its original name of *Ilhanung*. The representatives from all sections of the kingdom agreed and on the first day of autumn they celebrated again; the founding of the Kingdom of *Ilhanung*.

Simon and his crew set sail southward a few months after he arrived in the capital city. He came to visit his friends in Pujon before leaving; promising to return someday.

Wonjoon and Keeyun went back to school right after their adventures and waited patiently to finish their studies. Meantime Wonjoon and Jaeyin sent a few letters back and forth. Delivery was difficult and they sometimes did not arrive. Sensing that correspondence would remain difficult they both stopped; but still hoped to see each other again.

Life steadily improved in the whole kingdom the next year as the unified kingdom prospered.

ABOUT THE AUTHOR

Mark E. Verderame is a graduate from the Saint John's University in New York City. He has lived, worked, and studied on four continents. He enjoys learning about people of different backgrounds and cultures. But spending time with family and friends back home is his greatest reward and treasure in life.